Austin Dobson

Poems upon Several Occasions

Vol. II

Austin Dobson

Poems upon Several Occasions
Vol. II

ISBN/EAN: 9783744713276

Printed in Europe, USA, Canada, Australia, Japan

Cover: Foto ©Andreas Hilbeck / pixelio.de

More available books at **www.hansebooks.com**

POEMS

ON SEVERAL OCCASIONS

BY

AUSTIN DOBSON

NEW EDITION REVISED AND ENLARGED

𝔚ith 𝔦llustrations

IN TWO VOLUMES

Vol. II.

LONDON

KEGAN PAUL, TRENCH, TRÜBNER, & CO. Lᵀᴰ

MDCCCXCV

" At the Sign of the Lyre,"
Good Folk, we present you,
With the pick of our quire —
And we hope to content you !

Here be Ballad and Song,
The fruits of our leisure,
Some short and some long, —
May they all give you pleasure !

But if, when you read,
They should fail to restore you,
Farewell, and God-speed —
The world is before you !

CONTENTS.

----&----

vii

CONTENTS.

CONTENTS.

CONTENTS.

AT THE SIGN OF THE LYRE.

VOL. II. — I

THE LADIES OF ST. JAMES'S.

A PROPER NEW BALLAD OF THE COUNTRY AND THE TOWN.

" Phyllida amo ante alias."
VIRG.

THE ladies of St. James's
  Go swinging to the play;
Their footmen run before them,
  With a " Stand by! Clear the way! "
But Phyllida, my Phyllida!
  She takes her buckled shoon,
When we go out a-courting
  Beneath the harvest moon.

The ladies of St. James's
  Wear satin on their backs;
They sit all night at *Ombre*,
  With candles all of wax:
But Phyllida, my Phyllida!
  She dons her russet gown,
And runs to gather May dew
  Before the world is down.

The ladies of St. James's!
They are so fine and fair,
You 'd think a box of essences
Was broken in the air:
But Phyllida, my Phyllida!
The breath of heath and furze,
When breezes blow at morning,
Is not so fresh as hers.

The ladies of St. James's!
They 're painted to the eyes;
Their white it stays for ever,
Their red it never dies:
But Phyllida, my Phyllida!
Her colour comes and goes;
It trembles to a lily, —
It wavers to a rose.

The ladies of St. James's!
You scarce can understand
The half of all their speeches,
Their phrases are so grand:
But Phyllida, my Phyllida!
Her shy and simple words
Are clear as after rain-drops
The music of the birds.

4

The ladies of St. James's !
  They have their fits and freaks ;
They smile on you — for seconds,
  They frown on you — for weeks :
But Phyllida, my Phyllida !
  Come either storm or shine,
From Shrove-tide unto Shrove-tide,
  Is always true — and mine.

My Phyllida ! my Phyllida !
  I care not though they heap
The hearts of all St. James's,
  And give me all to keep ;
I care not whose the beauties
  Of all the world may be,
For Phyllida — for Phyllida
  Is all the world to me !

5

THE OLD SEDAN CHAIR.

"*What's not destroy'd by Time's devouring Hand?*
Where's Troy, and where's the May-Pole in the Strand?"
BRAMSTON'S "ART OF POLITICKS."

IT stands in the stable-yard, under the eaves,
    Propped up by a broom-stick and covered
      with leaves :
It once was the pride of the gay and the fair,
But now 'tis a ruin, — that old Sedan chair !

It is battered and tattered, — it little avails
That once it was lacquered, and glistened with
      nails ;
For its leather is cracked into lozenge and square,
Like a canvas by Wilkie, — that old Sedan chair !

See, — here came the bearing-straps ; here were
      the holes
For the poles of the bearers — when once there
      were poles ;
It was cushioned with silk, it was wadded with
      hair,
As the birds have discovered, — that old Sedan
      chair !

6

"Where's Troy?" says the poet! Look, —
    under the seat,
Is a nest with four eggs, — 'tis the favoured
    retreat
Of the Muscovy hen, who has hatched, I dare
    swear,
Quite an army of chicks in that old Sedan chair!

And yet — Can't you fancy a face in the frame
Of the window, — some high-headed damsel or
    dame,
Be-patched and be-powdered, just set by the
    stair,
While they raise up the lid of that old Sedan
    chair?

Can't you fancy Sir Plume, as beside her he
    stands,
With his ruffles a-droop on his delicate hands,
With his cinnamon coat, with his laced solitaire,
As he lifts her out light from that old Sedan chair?

Then it swings away slowly. Ah, many a league
It has trotted 'twixt sturdy-legged Terence and
    Teague;
Stout fellows! — but prone, on a question of fare,
To brandish the poles of that old Sedan chair!

It has waited by portals where Garrick has
    played ;
It has waited by Heidegger's " Grand Mas-
    querade ; "
For my Lady Codille, for my Lady Bellair,
It has waited — and waited, that old Sedan chair !

Oh, the scandals it knows ! Oh, the tales it could
    tell
Of Drum and Ridotto, of Rake and of Belle, —
Of Cock-fight and Levee, and (scarcely more
    rare !)
Of Fête-days at Tyburn, that old Sedan chair !

" *Heu ! quantum mutata,* " I say as I go.
It deserves better fate than a stable-yard, though !
We must furbish it up, and dispatch it, — " With
    Care," —
To a Fine-Art Museum — that old Sedan chair !

TO AN INTRUSIVE BUTTERFLY.

" Kill not — for Pity's sake — and lest ye slay
The meanest thing upon its upward way."
        FIVE RULES OF BUDDHA.

I WATCH you through the garden walks,
    I watch you float between
The avenues of dahlia stalks,
    And flicker on the green ;
You hover round the garden seat,
    You mount, you waver. Why, —
Why storm us in our still retreat,
    O saffron Butterfly !

Across the room in loops of flight
    I watch you wayward go ;
Dance down a shaft of glancing light,
    Review my books a-row ;
Before the bust you flaunt and flit
    Of " blind Mæonides " —
Ah, trifler, on his lips there lit
    Not butterflies, but bees !

9

You pause, you poise, you circle up
  Among my old Japan ;
You find a comrade on a cup,
  A friend upon a fan ;
You wind anon, a breathing-while,
  Around AMANDA's brow ; —
Dost dream her then, O Volatile !
  E'en such an one as thou ?

Away ! Her thoughts are not as thine.
  A sterner purpose fills
Her steadfast soul with deep design
  Of baby bows and frills ;
What care hath she for worlds without,
  What heed for yellow sun,
Whose endless hopes revolve about
  A planet, *ætat* One !

Away ! Tempt not the best of wives ;
  Let not thy garish wing
Come fluttering our Autumn lives
  With truant dreams of Spring !
Away ! Re-seek thy " Flowery Land ; "
  Be Buddha's law obeyed ;
Lest Betty's undiscerning hand
  Should slay . . . a future PRAED !

THE·CURÉ'S PROGRESS.

MONSIEUR the Curé down the street
Comes with his kind old face, —
With his coat worn bare, and his straggling hair,
And his green umbrella-case.

You may see him pass by the little *"Grande Place,"*
And the tiny *" Hôtel-de-Ville " ;*
He smiles, as he goes, to the *fleuriste* Rose,
And the *pompier* Théophile.

He turns, as a rule, through the *" Marché"* cool,
Where the noisy fish-wives call ;
And his compliment pays to the *" Belle Thérèse,"*
As she knits in her dusky stall.

There's a letter to drop at the locksmith's shop,
And Toto, the locksmith's niece,
Has jubilant hopes, for the Curé gropes
In his tails for a *pain d'épice.*

There's a little dispute with a merchant of fruit,
Who is said to be heterodox,

11

That will ended be with a " *Ma foi, oui !*"
And a pinch from the Curé's box.

There is also a word that no one heard
To the furrier's daughter Lou. ;
And a pale cheek fed with a flickering red,
And a " *Bon Dieu garde M'sieu !* "

But a grander way for the *Sous-Préfet,*
And a bow for Ma'am'selle Anne ;
And a mock " off-hat " to the Notary's cat,
And a nod to the Sacristan : —

For ever through life the Curé goes
With a smile on his kind old face —
With his coat worn bare, and his straggling hair,
And his green umbrella-case.

THE MASQUE OF THE MONTHS.

(FOR A FRESCO.)

FIRSTLY thou, churl son of Janus,
    Rough for cold, in drugget clad,
Com'st with rack and rheum to pain us ; —
Firstly thou, churl son of Janus.
Caverned now is old Sylvanus ;
    Numb and chill are maid and lad.

After thee thy dripping brother,
    Dank his weeds around him cling ;
Fogs his footsteps swathe and smother, —
After thee thy dripping brother.
Hearth-set couples hush each other,
    Listening for the cry of Spring.

Hark ! for March thereto doth follow,
    Blithe, — a herald tabarded ;
O'er him flies the shifting swallow, —
Hark ! for March thereto doth follow.
Swift his horn, by holt and hollow,
    Wakes the flowers in winter dead.

13

Thou then, April, Iris' daughter,
   Born between the storm and sun ;
Coy as nymph ere Pan hath caught her, —
Thou then, April, Iris' daughter.
Now are light, and rustling water ;
   Now are mirth, and nests begun.

May the jocund cometh after,
   Month of all the Loves (and mine) ;
Month of mock and cuckoo-laughter, —
May the jocund cometh after.
Beaks are gay on roof and rafter ;
   Luckless lovers peak and pine.

June the next, with roses scented,
   Languid from a slumber-spell ;
June in shade of leafage tented ; —
June the next, with roses scented.
Now her Itys, still lamented,
   Sings the mournful Philomel.

Hot July thereafter rages,
   Dog-star smitten, wild with heat ;
Fierce as pard the hunter cages, —
Hot July thereafter rages.
Traffic now no more engages ;
   Tongues are still in stall and street.

August next, with cider mellow,
   Laughs from out the poppied corn ;
Hook at back, a lusty fellow, —
August next, with cider mellow.
Now in wains the sheafage yellow
   'Twixt the hedges slow is borne.

Laden deep with fruity cluster,
   Then September, ripe and hale ;
Bees about his basket fluster, —
Laden deep with fruity cluster.
Skies have now a softer lustre ;
   Barns resound to flap of flail.

Thou then, too, of woodlands lover,
   Dusk October, berry-stained ;
Wailed about of parting plover, —
Thou then, too, of woodlands lover.
Fading now are copse and cover ;
   Forests now are sere and waned.

Next November, limping, battered,
   Blinded in a whirl of leaf ;
Worn of want and travel-tattered, —
Next November, limping, battered.
Now the goodly ships are shattered,
   Far at sea, on rock and reef.

Last of all the shrunk December
   Cowled for age, in ashen gray ;
Fading like a fading ember, —
Last of all the shrunk December.
Him regarding, men remember
   Life and joy must pass away.

TWO SERMONS.

BETWEEN the rail of woven brass,
    That hides the " Strangers' Pew,"
I hear the gray-haired vicar pass
    From Section One to Two.

And somewhere on my left I see —
    Whene'er I chance to look —
A soft-eyed, girl St. Cecily,
    Who notes them — in a book.

Ah, worthy GOODMAN, — sound divine !
    Shall I your wrath incur,
If I admit these thoughts of mine
    Will sometimes stray — to her ?

I know your theme, and I revere ;
    I hear your precepts tried ;
Must I confess I also hear
    A sermon at my side ?

Or how explain this need I feel, —
This impulse prompting me
Within my secret self to kneel
To Faith, — to Purity!

"AU REVOIR."

A Dramatic Vignette.

Scene.—*The Fountain in the Garden of the Lux-embourg. It is surrounded by Promenaders.*

Monsieur Jolicœur.   A Lady (*unknown*).

M. Jolicœur.
'TIS she, no doubt.   Brunette, — and tall :
    A charming figure, above all !
This promises. — Ahem !

The Lady.
        Monsieur ?
Ah ! it is three.   Then Monsieur's name
Is Jolicœur ? . . .

M. Jolicœur.
        Madame, the same.

The Lady.
And Monsieur's goodness has to say ? . . .
Your note ? . . .

19

M. JOLICŒUR.
Your note.

THE LADY.
Forgive me. — Nay.
(*Reads*)
"*If Madame* [I omit] *will be
Beside the Fountain-rail at Three,
Then Madame — possibly — may hear
News of her Spaniel.* JOLICŒUR."
Monsieur denies his note ?

M. JOLICŒUR.
I do.
Now let me read the one from you.
"*If Monsieur Jolicœur will be
Beside the Fountain-rail at Three.
Then Monsieur — possibly — may meet
An old Acquaintance.* 'INDISCREET.'"

THE LADY (*scandalized*).
Ah, what a folly ! 'Tis not true.
I never met Monsieur. And you ?

M. JOLICŒUR (*with gallantry*).
Have lived in vain till now. But see :
We are observed.

THE LADY (*looking round*).
          I comprehend . . .
     (*After a pause.*)
Monsieur, malicious brains combine
For your discomfiture, and mine.
Let us defeat that ill design.
If Monsieur but . . . (*hesitating*).

     M. JOLICŒUR (*bowing*).
          Rely on me.

     THE LADY (*still hesitating*).
Monsieur, I know, will understand . . .

     M. JOLICŒUR.
Madame, I wait but your command.

     THE LADY.
You are too good.   Then condescend
At once to be a new-found Friend !

M. JOLICŒUR (*entering upon the part forthwith*).
How ? I am charmed, — enchanted.   Ah !
What ages since we met . . . at *Spa* ?

     THE LADY (*a little disconcerted*).
At *Ems*, I think.   Monsieur, maybe,
Will recollect the Orangery ?

21

M. JOLICŒUR.

At *Ems*, of course.   But Madame's face
Might make one well forget a place.

THE LADY.

It seems so.   Still, Monsieur recalls
The Kürhaus, and the concert-balls?

M. JOLICŒUR.

Assuredly.   Though there again
'Tis Madame's image I retain.

THE LADY.

Monsieur is skilled in . . . repartee.
(How do they take it? — Can you see?)

M. JOLICŒUR.

Nay, — Madame furnishes the wit.
(They don't know what to make of it!)

THE LADY.

And Monsieur's friend who sometimes came? . .
That clever . . . I forget the name.

M. JOLICŒUR.

The BARON? . . . It escapes me, too.
'Twas doubtless he that Madame knew?

THE LADY (*archly*).
Precisely.   But, my carriage waits.
Monsieur will see me to the gates ?

M. JOLICŒUR (*offering his arm*).
I shall be charmed.   (Your stratagem
Bids fair, I think, to conquer them.)
                                        (*Aside*)
(Who is she ?   I must find that out.)
— And Madame's husband thrives, no doubt ?

THE LADY (*off her guard*).
Monsieur de BEAU — ? . . He died at *Dôle !*

M. JOLICŒUR.
Truly.   How sad !
                  (*Aside*)
                  (Yet, on the whole,
How fortunate !   BEAU-*pré* ? — BEAU-*vau* ?
Which can it be ?   Ah, there they go !)
— Madame, your enemies retreat
With all the honours of . . . defeat.

THE LADY.
Thanks to Monsieur.   Monsieur has shown
A skill PRÉVILLE could not disown.

23

M. JOLICŒUR.

You flatter me.   We need no skill
To act so nearly what we will.
Nay, — what may come to pass, if Fate
And Madame bid me cultivate . . .

THE LADY (*anticipating*).

Alas ! — no farther than the gate.
Monsieur, besides, is too polite
To profit by a jest so slight.

M. JOLICŒUR.

Distinctly.   Still, I did but glance
At possibilities . . . of Chance.

THE LADY.

Which must not serve Monsieur, I fear,
Beyond the little grating here.

M. JOLICŒUR (*aside*).

(She 's perfect.   One may push too far,
Piano, sano.)
        (*They reach the gates.*)
            Here we are.
Permit me, then . . .
        (*Placing her in the carriage.*)
                And Madame goes? . . .
Your coachman ? . . . Can I ? . . .

24

THE LADY (*smiling*).
Thanks! he knows.
Thanks! Thanks!

M. JOLICŒUR (*insidiously*).
And shall we not renew
Our . . . " *Ems* acquaintanceship ? "

THE LADY (*still smiling*).
Adieu !
My thanks instead !

M. JOLICŒUR (*with pathos*).
It is too hard !
(*Laying his hand on the grating.*)
To find one's Paradise is barred ! !

THE LADY.
Nay. — " Virtue is her own Reward ! "
[*Exit.*

M. JOLICŒUR (*solus*).
BEAU-*vau* ? — BEAU-*vallon* ? — BEAU-*manoir*? —
But that 's a detail !
(*Waving his hand after the carriage.*)
AU REVOIR !

THE CARVER AND THE CALIPH.

(WE lay our story in the East.
Because 'tis Eastern? Not the least.
We place it there because we fear
To bring its parable too near,
And seem to touch with impious hand
Our dear, confiding native land.)

HAROUN ALRASCHID, in the days
He went about his vagrant ways,
And prowled at eve for good or bad
In lanes and alleys of BAGDAD,
Once found, at edge of the bazaar,
E'en where the poorest workers are,
A Carver.

Fair his work and fine
With mysteries of inlaced design,
And shapes of shut significance
To aught but an anointed glance, —
The dreams and visions that grow plain
In darkened chambers of the brain.

26

And all day busily he wrought
From dawn to eve, but no one bought ; —
Save when some Jew with look askant,
Or keen-eyed Greek from the Levant,
Would pause awhile, — depreciate, —
Then buy a month's work by the weight,
Bearing it swiftly over seas
To garnish rich men's treasuries.

And now for long none bought at all,
So lay he sullen in his stall.
Him thus withdrawn the Caliph found,
And smote his staff upon the ground —
" Ho, there, within I   Hast wares to sell ?
Or slumber'st, having dined too well ? "
" ' Dined,' " quoth the man, with sullen eyes,
" How should I dine when no one buys ? "
"Nay," said the other, answering low, —
" Nay, I but jested.   Is it so ?
Take then this coin, . . but take beside
A counsel, friend, thou hast not tried.
This craft of thine, the mart to suit,
Is too refined, — remote, — minute ;
These small conceptions can but fail ;
'Twere best to work on larger scale,
And rather choose such themes as wear
More of the earth and less of air,

The fisherman that hauls his net, —
The merchants in the market set, —
The couriers posting in the street, —
The gossips as they pass and greet, —
These — these are clear to all men's eyes,
Therefore with these they sympathize.
Further (neglect not this advice !)
Be sure to ask three times the price."

The Carver sadly shook his head ;
He knew 'twas truth the Caliph said.
From that day forth his work was planned
So that the world might understand.
He carved it deeper, and more plain ;
He carved it thrice as large again ;
He sold it, too, for thrice the cost ;
— Ah, but the Artist that was lost !

TO AN UNKNOWN BUST IN THE BRITISH MUSEUM.

" Sermons in stones."

WHO were you once ?   Could we but guess,
  We might perchance more boldly
Define the patient weariness
  That sets your lips so coldly ;
You " lived," we know, for blame and fame ;
  But sure, to friend or foeman,
You bore some more distinctive name
  Than mere " B. C.,"— and " Roman " ?

Your pedestal should help us much.
  Thereon your acts, your title,
(Secure from cold Oblivion's touch !)
  Had doubtless due recital ;
Vain hope !— not even deeds can last !
  That stone, of which you 're *minus,*
Maybe with all your virtues past
  Endows . . a TIGELLINUS !

29

We seek it not ; we should not find.
  But still, it needs no magic
To tell you wore, like most mankind,
  Your comic mask and tragic ;
And held that things were false and true,
  Felt angry or forgiving,
As step by step you stumbled through
  This life-long task . . of living !

You tried the *cul-de-sac* of Thought ;
  The *montagne Russe* of Pleasure ;
You found the best Ambition brought
  Was strangely short of measure ;
You watched, at last, the fleet days fly,
  Till — drowsier and colder —
You felt MERCURIUS loitering by
  To touch you on the shoulder.

'Twas then (why not ?) the whim would come
  That howso Time should garble
Those deeds of yours when you were dumb,
  At least you 'd live — in Marble ;
You smiled to think that after days,
  At least, in Bust or Statue,
(We all have sick-bed dreams!) would gaze,
  Not quite incurious, at you.

30

We gaze ; *we* pity you, be sure !
   In truth, Death's worst inaction
Must be less tedious to endure
   Than nameless petrifaction ;
Far better, in some nook unknown,
   To sleep for once — and soundly,
Than still survive in wistful stone,
   Forgotten more profoundly !

MOLLY TREFUSIS.

"Now the Graces are four and the Venuses two,
And ten is the number of Muses;
For a Muse and a Grace and a Venus are you,—
My dear little Molly Trefusis!"

SO he wrote, the old bard of an "old magazine:"
   As a study it not without use is,
If we wonder a moment who she may have been,
   This same "little Molly Trefusis!"

She was Cornish. We know that at once by the
     " Tre ; "
Then of guessing it scarce an abuse is
If we say that where Bude bellows back to the sea
   Was the birthplace of Molly Trefusis.

And she lived in the era of patches and bows,
   Not knowing what rouge or ceruse is ;
For they needed (I trust) but her natural rose,
   The lilies of Molly Trefusis.

And I somehow connect her (I frankly admit
   That the evidence hard to produce is)

With BATH in its hey-day of Fashion and Wit, —
This dangerous Molly Trefusis.

I fancy her, radiant in ribbon and knot,
(How charming that old-fashioned puce is !)
All blooming in laces, fal-lals and what not,
At the PUMP ROOM, — Miss Molly Trefusis.

I fancy her reigning, — a Beauty, — a Toast,
Where BLADUD's medicinal cruse is ;
And we know that at least of one Bard it could
boast, —
The Court of Queen Molly Trefusis.

He says she was " VENUS." I doubt it. Beside,
(Your rhymer so hopelessly loose is !)
His " little " could scarce be to Venus applied,
If fitly to Molly Trefusis.

No, no. It was HEBE he had in his mind ;
And fresh as the handmaid of Zeus is,
And rosy, and rounded, and dimpled, — you 'll
find, —
Was certainly Molly Trefusis !

Then he calls her "a MUSE."   To the charge I
   reply
  That we all of us know what a Muse is ;
It is something too awful, — too acid, — too dry, —
  For sunny-eyed Molly Trefusis.

But "a GRACE."   There I grant he was probably
   right ;
  (The rest but a verse-making ruse is)
It was all that was graceful, — intangible, — light,
  The beauty of Molly Trefusis !

Was she wooed ?   Who can hesitate much about
   that
  Assuredly more than obtuse is ;
For how could the poet have written so pat
  "*My* dear little Molly Trefusis !"

And was wed ?   That I think we must plainly
   infer,
  Since of suitors the common excuse is
To take to them Wives.   So it happened to her,
  Of course, — "little Molly Trefusis !"

To the Bard ?   'Tis unlikely.   Apollo, you see,
  In practical matters a goose is ; —

'Twas a knight of the shire, and a hunting J.P.,
 Who carried off Molly Trefusis !

And you 'll find, I conclude, in the "*Gentleman's
  Mag.,*"
 At the end, where the pick of the news is,
"*On the* (blank), *at ' the Bath,' to Sir Hilary
  Bragg,*
 With a Fortune, Miss Molly Trefusis."

Thereupon . . But no farther the student may pry:
 Love's temple is dark as Eleusis ;
So here, at the threshold, we part, you and I,
 From "dear little Molly Trefusis."

AT THE CONVENT GATE.

WISTARIA blossoms trail and fall
　　Above the length of barrier wall ;
　　　And softly, now and then,
The shy, staid-breasted doves will flit
From roof to gateway-top, and sit
　　　And watch the ways of men.

The gate 's ajar.　If one might peep !
Ah, what a haunt of rest and sleep
　　　The shadowy garden seems !
And note how dimly to and fro
The grave, gray-hooded Sisters go,
　　　Like figures seen in dreams.

Look, there is one that tells her beads ;
And yonder one apart that reads
　　　A tiny missal's page ;
And see, beside the well, the two
That, kneeling. strive to lure anew
　　　The magpie to its cage !

36

Not beautiful — not all !   But each
With that mild grace, outlying speech,
    Which comes of even mood ; —
The Veil unseen that women wear
With heart-whole thought, and quiet care,
    And hope of higher good.

"A placid life — a peaceful life !
What need to these the name of Wife ?
    What gentler task (I said) —
What worthier — e'en your arts among —
Than tend the sick, and teach the young,
    And give the hungry bread ?"

" No worthier task ! " re-echoes She,
Who (closelier clinging) turns with me
    To face the road again :
— And yet, in that warm heart of hers,
She means the doves', for she prefers
    To "watch the ways of men."

THE MILKMAID.

A NEW SONG TO AN OLD TUNE.

ACROSS the grass I see her pass;
  She comes with tripping pace, —
A maid I know, — and March winds blow
  Her hair across her face; —
    With a hey, Dolly! ho, Dolly!
     Dolly shall be mine,
    Before the spray is white with May,
    Or blooms the eglantine.

The March winds blow. I watch her go:
  Her eye is brown and clear;
Her cheek is brown, and soft as down,
  (To those who see it near!) —
    With a hey, Dolly! ho, Dolly!
     Dolly shall be mine,
    Before the spray is white with May,
    Or blooms the eglantine.

What has she not that those have got, —
  The dames that walk in silk!

If she undo her 'kerchief blue,
   Her neck is white as milk.
      With a hey, Dolly! ho, Dolly!
        Dolly shall be mine,
      Before the spray is white with May,
      Or blooms the eglantine.

Let those who will be proud and chill!
   For me, from June to June,
My Dolly's words are sweet as curds —
   Her laugh is like a tune; —
      With a hey, Dolly! ho, Dolly!
        Dolly shall be mine,
      Before the spray is white with May,
      Or blooms the eglantine.

Break, break to hear, O crocus-spear!
   O tall Lent-lilies flame!
There'll be a bride at Easter-tide,
   And Dolly is her name.
      With a hey, Dolly! ho, Dolly!
        Dolly shall be mine,
     Before the spray is white with May,
      Or blooms the eglantine.

AN OLD FISH POND.

GREEN growths of mosses drop and bead
    Around the granite brink ;
And 'twixt the isles of water-weed
    The wood-birds dip and drink.

Slow efts about the edges sleep ;
    Swift-darting water-flies
Shoot on the surface ; down the deep
    Fast-following bubbles rise.

Look down.   What groves that scarcely sway !
    What " wood obscure," profound !
What jungle ! — where some beast of prey
    Might choose his vantage-ground !
    *   *   *   *   *

Who knows what lurks beneath the tide ? —
    Who knows what tale ?   Belike,
Those " antres vast " and shadows hide
    Some patriarchal Pike ; —

Some tough old tyrant, wrinkle-jawed,
    To whom the sky, the earth,

Have but for aim to look on awed
  And see him wax in girth ; —

Hard ruler there by right of might ;
  An ageless Autocrat,
Whose " good old rule " is " Appetite,
  And subjects fresh and fat ; " —

While they — poor souls ! — in wan despair
  Still watch for signs in him ;
And dying, hand from heir to heir
  The day undawned and dim,

When the pond's terror too must go ;
  Or creeping in by stealth,
Some bolder brood, with common blow,
  Shall found a Commonwealth.

        *   *   *   *   *

Or say, — perchance the liker this ! —
  That these themselves are gone ;
That Amurath *in minimis*, —
  Still hungry, — lingers on,

With dwindling trunk and wolfish jaw
  Revolving sullen things,
But most the blind unequal law
  That rules the food of Kings ; —

The blot that makes the cosmic All
A mere time-honoured cheat ; —
That bids the Great to eat the Small,
Yet lack the Small to eat !

     *   *   *   *   *

Who knows ! Meanwhile the mosses bead
Around the granite brink ;
And 'twixt the isles of water-weed
The wood-birds dip and drink.

AN EASTERN APOLOGUE.

(To E. H. P.)

MELIK the Sultán, tired and wan,
Nodded at noon on his diván.

Beside the fountain lingered near
JAMÍL the bard, and the vizier —

Old YÚSUF, sour and hard to please ;
Then JAMÍL sang, in words like these.

Slim is Butheina — slim is she
As boughs of the Aráka tree !

" Nay," quoth the other, teeth between,
" Lean, if you will, — I call her lean."

Sweet is Butheina — sweet as wine,
With smiles that like red bubbles shine !

" True, — by the Prophet ! " YÚSUF said.
" She makes men wander in the head ! "

43

Dear is Bútheina — ah! more dear
Than all the maidens of Kashmeer!

" Dear," came the answer, quick as thought,
" Dear . . and yet always to be bought."

So JAMÍL ceased.   But still Life's page
Shows diverse unto YOUTH and AGE :

And, — be the song of Ghouls or Gods, —
TIME, like the Sultán, sits . . and nods.

TO A MISSAL OF THE THIRTEENTH CENTURY.

M ISSAL of the Gothic age,
    Missal with the blazoned page,
Whence, O Missal, hither come,
From what dim scriptorium?

Whose the name that wrought thee thus,
Ambrose or Theophilus,
Bending, through the waning light,
O'er thy vellum scraped and white;

Weaving 'twixt thy rubric lines
Sprays and leaves and quaint designs;
Setting round thy border scrolled
Buds of purple and of gold?

Ah! — a wondering brotherhood,
Doubtless, by that artist stood,
Raising o'er his careful ways
Little choruses of praise;

45

Glad when his deft hand would paint
Strife of Sathanas and Saint,
Or in secret coign entwist
Jest of cloister humourist.

Well the worker earned his wage,
Bending o'er the blazoned page !
Tired the hand and tired the wit
Ere the final *Explicit !*

Not as ours the books of old —
Things that steam can stamp and fold ;
Not as ours the books of yore —
Rows of type, and nothing more.

Then a book was still a Book,
Where a wistful man might look,
Finding something through the whole,
Beating — like a human soul.

In that growth of day by day,
When to labour was to pray,
Surely something vital passed
To the patient page at last ;

46

TO A MISSAL.

Something that one still perceives
Vaguely present in the leaves ;
Something from the worker lent ;
Something mute — but eloquent !

A REVOLUTIONARY RELIC.

OLD it is, and worn and battered,
    As I lift it from the stall ;
And the leaves are frayed and tattered,
And the pendent sides are shattered,
    Pierced and blackened by a ball.

'Tis the tale of grief and gladness
    Told by sad St. Pierre of yore,
That in front of France's madness
Hangs a strange seductive sadness,
    Grown pathetic evermore.

And a perfume round it hovers,
    Which the pages half reveal,
For a folded corner covers,
Interlaced, two names of lovers, —
    A " Savignac " and " Lucile."

As I read I marvel whether,
    In some pleasant old château,
Once they read this book together,
In the scented summer weather,
    With the shining Loire below ?

48

Nooked — secluded from espial,
　Did Love slip and snare them so,
While the hours danced round the dial
To the sound of flute and viol,
　In that pleasant old château?

Did it happen that no single
　Word of mouth could either speak?
Did the brown and gold hair mingle,
Did the shamed skin thrill and tingle
　To the shock of cheek and cheek?

Did they feel with that first flushing
　Some new sudden power to feel,
Some new inner spring set gushing
At the names together rushing
　Of "Savignac" and "Lucile"?

Did he drop on knee before her —
　"*Son Amour, son Cœur, sa Reine*" —
In his high-flown way adore her,
Urgent, eloquent implore her,
　Plead his pleasure and his pain?

Did she turn with sight swift-dimming,
　And the quivering lip we know,
With the full, slow eyelid brimming,

With the languorous pupil swimming,
   Like the love of Mirabeau ?

Stretch her hand from cloudy frilling,
   For his eager lips to press ;
In a flash all fate fulfilling
Did he catch her, trembling, thrilling —
   Crushing life to one caress ?

Did they sit in that dim sweetness
   Of attained love's after-calm,
Marking not the world — its meetness,
Marking Time not, nor his fleetness,
   Only happy, palm to palm ?

Till at last she, — sunlight smiting
   Red on wrist and cheek and hair, —
Sought the page where love first lighting,
Fixed their fate, and, in this writing,
   Fixed the record of it there.

   *   *   *   *

Did they marry midst the smother,
   Shame and slaughter of it all ?
Did she wander like that other
Woful, wistful, wife and mother,
   Round and round his prison wall ; —

Wander wailing, as the plover
  Waileth, wheeleth, desolate,
Heedless of the hawk above her,
While as yet the rushes cover,
  Waning fast, her wounded mate ; —

Wander, till his love's eyes met hers,
  Fixed and wide in their despair?
Did he burst his prison fetters,
Did he write sweet, yearning letters,
  " *A Lucile, — en Angleterre* " ?

Letters where the reader, reading,
  Halts him with a sudden stop,
For he feels a man's heart bleeding,
Draining out its pain's exceeding —
  Half a life, at every drop :

Letters where Love's iteration
  Seems to warble and to rave ;
Letters where the pent sensation
Leaps to lyric exultation,
  Like a song-bird from a grave.

Where, through Passion's wild repeating,
  Peep the Pagan and the Gaul,
Politics and love competing,

51

Abelard and Cato greeting,
  Rousseau ramping over all.

Yet your critic's right — you waive it,
  Whirled along the fever-flood ;
And its touch of truth shall save it,
And its tender rain shall lave it,
For at least you read *Amavit*,
  Written there in tears of blood.

    *   *   *   *   *

Did they hunt him to his hiding,
  Tracking traces in the snow ?
Did they tempt him out, confiding,
Shoot him ruthless down, deriding,
  By the ruined old château ?

Left to lie, with thin lips resting
  Frozen to a smile of scorn,
Just the bitter thought's suggesting,
At this excellent new jesting
  Of the rabble Devil-born.

Till some "tiger-monkey," finding
  These few words the covers bear,
Some swift rush of pity blinding,
Sent them in the shot-pierced binding
  "*A Lucile, en Angleterre.*"

    *   *   *   *   *

Fancies only! Nought the covers,
  Nothing more the leaves reveal,
Yet I love it for its lovers,
For the dream that round it hovers
  Of "Savignac" and "Lucile."

A MADRIGAL.

BEFORE me, careless lying,
　　Young Love his ware comes crying;
Full soon the elf untreasures
His pack of pains and pleasures, —
　　With roguish eye,
　　He bids me buy
From out his pack of treasures.

His wallet's stuffed with blisses,
With true-love-knots and kisses,
With rings and rosy fetters,
And sugared vows and letters ; —
　　He holds them out
　　With boyish flout,
And bids me try the fetters.

Nay, Child (I cry), I know them ;
There's little need to show them !
Too well for new believing
I know their past deceiving, —
　　I am too old
　　(I say), and cold,
To-day, for new believing !

54

But still the wanton presses,
With honey-sweet caresses,
And still, to my undoing,
He wins me, with his wooing,
 To buy his ware
 With all its care,
Its sorrow and undoing.

A SONG TO THE LUTE.

WHEN first I came to Court,
      Fa la!
When first I came to Court,
I deemed Dan Cupid but a boy,
And Love an idle sport,
A sport whereat a man might toy
With little hurt and mickle joy —
When first I came to Court !

Too soon I found my fault,
      Fa la!
Too soon I found my fault ;
The fairest of the fair brigade
Advanced to mine assault.
Alas ! against an adverse maid
Nor fosse can serve nor palisade —
Too soon I found my fault !

When SILVIA's eyes assail,
      Fa la!
When SILVIA's eyes assail,
No feint the arts of war can show,

No counterstroke avail ;
Naught skills but arms away to throw,
And kneel before that lovely foe,
When SILVIA's eyes assail !

Yet is all truce in vain,
    Fa la !
Yet is all truce in vain,
Since she that spares doth still pursue
To vanquish once again ;
And naught remains for man to do
But fight once more, to yield anew,
And so all truce is vain !

A GARDEN SONG.

(To W. E. H.)

H ERE, in this sequestered close
    Bloom the hyacinth and rose ;
Here beside the modest stock
Flaunts the flaring hollyhock ;
Here, without a pang, one sees
Ranks, conditions, and degrees.

All the seasons run their race
In this quiet resting place ;
Peach, and apricot, and fig
Here will ripen, and grow big ;
Here is store and overplus, —
More had not Alcinoüs !

Here, in alleys cool and green,
Far ahead the thrush is seen ;
Here along the southern wall
Keeps the bee his festival ;
All is quiet else — afar
Sounds of toil and turmoil are.

58

Here be shadows large and long;
Here be spaces meet for song;
Grant, O garden-god, that I,
Now that none profane is nigh, —
Now that mood and moment please,
Find the fair Pierides !

A CHAPTER OF FROISSART.

(GRANDPAPA LOQUITUR.)

YOU don't know Froissart now, young folks.
 This age, I think, prefers recitals
Of high-spiced crime, with " slang " for jokes,
  And startling titles ;

But, in my time, when still some few
 Loved " old Montaigne," and praised Pope's
  Homer
(Nay, thought to style him " poet " too,
  Were scarce misnomer),

Sir John was less ignored. Indeed,
 I can re-call how Some-one present
(Who spoils her grandson, Frank !) would read,
  And find him pleasant ;

For, — by this copy, — hangs a Tale.
 Long since, in an old house in Surrey,
Where men knew more of " morning ale "
  Than " Lindley Murray,"

In a dim-lighted, whip-hung hall,
  'Neath Hogarth's "Midnight Conversation,"
It stood ; and oft 'twixt spring and fall,
    With fond elation,

I turned the brown old leaves. For there
  All through one hopeful happy summer,
At such a page (I well knew where),
    Some secret comer,

Whom I can picture, 'Trix, like you
  (Though scarcely such a colt unbroken),
Would sometimes place for private view
    A certain token ; —

A rose-leaf meaning " Garden Wall,"
  An ivy-leaf for " Orchard corner,"
A thorn to say " Don't come at all," —
    Unwelcome warner ! —

Not that, in truth, our friends gainsaid ;
  But then Romance required dissembling,
(Ann Radcliffe taught us that !) which bred
    Some genuine trembling ;

Though, as a rule, all used to end
  In such kind confidential parley
As may to you kind Fortune send,
      You long-legged Charlie,

When your time comes.   How years slip on !
  We had our crosses like our betters ;
Fate sometimes looked askance upon
      Those floral letters ;

And once, for three long days disdained,
  The dust upon the folio settled ;
For some-one, in the right, was pained,
      And some-one nettled,

That sure was in the wrong, but spake
  Of fixed intent and purpose stony
To serve King George, enlist and make
      Minced-meat of " Boney,"

Who yet survived — ten years at least.
  And so, when she I mean came hither,
One day that need for letters ceased,
      She brought this with her !

Here is the leaf-stained Chapter : — *How*
  The English King laid Siege to Calais ;
I think Gran. knows it even now, —
        Go ask her, Alice.
        .

TO THE MAMMOTH-TORTOISE

OF THE MASCARENE ISLANDS.

" *Tuque, Testudo, resonare septem*
Callida nervis."

HOR. iii. II.

MONSTER Chelonian, you suggest
   To some, no doubt, the calm, —
The torpid ease of islets drest
   In fan-like fern and palm ;

To some your cumbrous ways, perchance,
   Darwinian dreams recall ;
And some your Rip-van-Winkle glance,
   And ancient youth appal ;

So widely varied views dispose :
   But not so mine, — for me
Your vasty vault but simply shows
   A LYRE immense, *per se*,

A LYRE to which the Muse might chant
   A truly " Orphic tale,"
Could she but find that public want,
   A Bard — of equal scale !

64

Oh, for a Bard of awful words,
  And lungs serenely strong,
To sweep from your sonorous chords
  Niagaras of song,

Till, dinned by that tremendous strain,
  The grovelling world aghast,
Should leave its paltry greed of gain,
  And mend its ways . . . at last !

A ROMAN "ROUND-ROBIN."

("HIS FRIENDS" TO QUINTUS HORATIUS FLACCUS.)

"*Hæc decies repetita* [non] *placebit.*" — ARS POETICA.

FLACCUS, you write us charming songs:
    No bard we know possesses
In such perfection what belongs
    To brief and bright addresses;

No man can say that Life is short
    With mien so little fretful;
No man to Virtue's paths exhort
    In phrases less regretful;

Or touch, with more serene distress,
    On Fortune's ways erratic;
And then delightfully digress
    From Alp to Adriatic:

All this is well, no doubt, and tends
    Barbarian minds to soften;
But, HORACE — we, we are your friends —
    Why tell *us* this so often?

66

Why feign to spread a cheerful feast,
  And then thrust in our faces
These barren scraps (to say the least)
  Of Stoic common-places ?

Recount, and welcome, your pursuits :
  Sing Lydë's lyre and hair ;
Sing drums and Berecynthian flutes ;
  Sing parsley-wreaths ; but spare, —

O, spare to sing, what none deny,
  That things we love decay ; —
That Time and Gold have wings to fly ; —
  That all must Fate obey !

Or bid us dine — on this day week —
  And pour us, if you can,
As soft and sleek as girlish cheek,
  Your inmost Cæcuban ; —

Of that we fear not overplus ;
  But your didactic ' tap '—
Forgive us ! — grows monotonous ;
  Nunc vale ! Verbum sap.

VERSES TO ORDER.

(FOR A DRAWING BY E. A. ABBEY.)

HOW weary 'twas to wait !   The year
    Went dragging slowly on ;
The red leaf to the running brook
    Dropped sadly, and was gone ;
December came, and locked in ice
    The plashing of the mill ;
The white snow filled the orchard up ;
    But she was waiting still.

Spring stirred and broke.   The rooks once more
    'Gan cawing in the loft ;
The young lambs' new awakened cries
    Came trembling from the croft ;
The clumps of primrose filled again
    The hollows by the way ;
The pale wind-flowers blew ; but she
    Grew paler still than they.

How weary 'twas to wait !   With June,
    Through all the drowsy street,

Came distant murmurs of the war,
   And rumours of the fleet ;
The gossips, from the market-stalls,
   Cried news of Joe and Tim ;
But June shed all her leaves, and still
   There came no news of him.

And then, at last, at last, at last,
   One blessèd August morn,
Beneath the yellowing autumn elms,
   Pang-panging came the horn ;
The swift coach paused a creaking-space,
   Then flashed away, and passed ;
But she stood trembling yet, and dazed :
   The news had come — at last !

And thus the artist saw her stand,
   While all around her seems
As vague and shadowy as the shapes
   That flit from us in dreams ;
And naught in all the world is true,
   Save those few words which tell
That he she lost is found again —
   Is found again—and well !

A LEGACY.

AH, Postumus, we all must go :
   This keen North-Easter nips my shoulder ;
My strength begins to fail ; I know
   You find me older ;

I 've made my Will. Dear, faithful friend —
   My Muse's friend and not my purse's !
Who still would hear and still commend
   My tedious verses,

How will you live — of these deprived ?
   I've learned your candid soul. The venal, —
The sordid friend had scarce survived
   A test so penal ;

But you — Nay, nay, 'tis so. The rest
   Are not as you : you hide your merit ;
You, more than all, deserve the best
   True friends inherit ; —

Not gold, — that hearts like yours despise ;
   Not " spacious dirt " (your own expression),

70

No ; but the rarer, dearer prize —
  The Life's Confession !

You catch my thought ? What ! Can't you guess ?
  You, you alone, admired my Cantos ; —
I've left you, P., my whole MS.,
  In three portmanteaus !

"LITTLE BLUE-RIBBONS."

"LITTLE Blue-Ribbons!" We call her that
 From the ribbons she wears in her fa-
  vourite hat;
For may not a person be only five,
And yet have the neatest of taste alive?—
As a matter of fact, this one has views
Of the strictest sort as to frocks and shoes;
And we never object to a sash or bow,
When "little Blue-Ribbons" prefers it so.

" Little Blue-Ribbons " has eyes of blue,
And an arch little mouth, when the teeth peep
  through;
And her primitive look is wise and grave,
With a sense of the weight of the word " behave;"
Though now and again she may condescend
To a radiant smile for a private friend;
But to smile for ever is weak, you know,
And "little Blue-Ribbons " regards it so.

She's a staid little woman! And so as well
Is her ladyship's doll, " Miss Bonnibelle;"

But I think what at present the most takes up
The thoughts of her heart is her last new cup ;
For the object thereon, — be it understood, —
Is the " Robin that buried the ' Babes in the
    Wood ' " —
It is not in the least like a robin, though,
But " little Blue-Ribbons " declares it so.

" Little Blue-Ribbons " believes, I think,
That the rain comes down for the birds to drink ;
Moreover, she holds, in a cab you'd get
To the spot where the suns of yesterday set ;
And I know that she fully expects to meet
With a lion or wolf in Regent Street !
We may smile, and deny as we like — But, no ;
For " little Blue-Ribbons " still dreams it so.

Dear " little Blue-Ribbons ! "   She tells us all
That she never intends to be "great" and "tall" ;
(For how could she ever contrive to sit
In her " own, own chair," if she grew one bit !)
And, further, she says, she intends to stay
In her "darling home" till she gets "quite gray ; "
Alas ! we are gray ; and we doubt, you know,
But " little Blue-Ribbons " will have it so !

LINES TO A STUPID PICTURE.

"— the music of the moon
Sleeps in the plain eggs of the nightingale."
AYLMER'S FIELD.

FIVE geese, — a landscape damp and wild, —
   A stunted, not too pretty, child,
   Beneath a battered gingham ;
Such things, to say the least, require
A Muse of more-than-average Fire
   Effectively to sing 'em.

And yet — Why should they ?   Souls of mark
Have sprung from such ; — e'en Joan of Arc
   Had scarce a grander duty ;
Not always ('tis a maxim trite)
From righteous sources comes the right, —
   From beautiful, the beauty.

Who shall decide where seed is sown ?
Maybe some priceless germ was blown
   To this unwholesome marish ;
(And what must grow will still increase,
Though cackled round by half the geese
   And ganders in the parish.)

Maybe this homely face may hide
A Staël before whose mannish pride
    Our frailer sex shall tremble ;
Perchance this audience anserine
May hiss (O fluttering Muse of mine !) —
    May hiss — a future Kemble !

Or say the gingham shadows o'er
An undeveloped Hannah More ! —
    A latent Mrs. Trimmer ! !
Who shall affirm it ? — who deny ? —
Since of the truth nor you nor I
    Discern the faintest glimmer ?

So then — Caps off, my Masters all ;
Reserve your final word, — recall
    Your all-too-hasty strictures ;
Caps off, I say, for Wisdom sees
Undreamed potentialities
    In most unhopeful pictures.

A FAIRY TALE.

" On court, hélas ! après la vérité ;
Ah ! croyez-moi, l'erreur a son mérite."
VOLTAIRE.

CURLED in a maze of dolls and bricks,
   I find Miss Mary, *ætat* six,
Blonde, blue-eyed, frank, capricious,
Absorbed in her first fairy book,
From which she scarce can pause to look,
   Because it's " *so* delicious ! "

" Such marvels, too.   A wondrous Boat,
In which they cross a magic Moat,
   That's smooth as glass to row on —
A Cat that brings all kinds of things ;
And see, the Queen has angel wings —
   Then OGRE comes " — and so on.

What trash it is !   How sad to find
(Dear Moralist !) the childish mind,
   So active and so pliant,
Rejecting themes in which you mix
Fond truths and pleasing facts, to fix
   On tales of Dwarf and Giant !

76

In merest prudence men should teach
That cats mellifluous in speech
   Are painful contradictions ;
That science ranks as monstrous things
Two pairs of upper limbs ; so wings —
   E'en angels' wings ! — are fictions :

That there's no giant now but Steam ;
That life, although "an empty dream,"
   Is scarce a "land of Fairy."
"Of course I said all this ? "   Why, no ;
I *did* a thing far wiser, though, —
   I read the tale with Mary.

TO A CHILD.

(FROM THE " GARLAND OF RACHEL.")

HOW shall I sing you, Child, for whom
　　So many lyres are strung ;
Or how the only tone assume
　　That fits a Maid so young ?

What rocks there are on either hand !
　　Suppose — 'tis on the cards —
You should grow up with quite a grand
　　Platonic hate for bards !

How shall I then be shamed, undone,
　　For ah ! with what a scorn
Your eyes must greet that luckless One
　　Who rhymed you, newly born, —

Who o'er your " helpless cradle " bent
　　His idle verse to turn ;
And twanged his tiresome instrument
　　Above your unconcern !

78

Nay, — let my words be so discreet,
   That, keeping Chance in view,
Whatever after fate you meet
   A part may still be true.

Let others wish you mere good looks, —
   Your sex is always fair ;
Or to be writ in Fortune's books, —
   She's rich who has to spare :

I wish you but a heart that 's kind,
   A head that's sound and clear ;
(Yet let the heart be not too blind,
   The head not too severe !)

A joy of life, a frank delight ;
   A not-too-large desire ;
And — if you fail to find a Knight —
   At least . . a trusty Squire.

HOUSEHOLD ART.

" MINE be a cot," for the hours of play,
  Of the kind that is built by Miss GREEN-
   AWAY ;
Where the walls are low, and the roofs are red,
And the birds are gay in the blue o'erhead ;
And the dear little figures, in frocks and frills,
Go roaming about at their own sweet wills,
And " play with the pups," and "reprove the
   calves,"
And do nought in the world (but Work) by halves,
From " Hunt the Slipper " and " Riddle-me-ree "
To watching the cat in the apple-tree.

O Art of the Household ! Men may prate
Of their ways " intense " and Italianate, —
They may soar on their wings of sense, and float
To the *au delà* and the dim remote, —
Till the last sun sink in the last-lit West,
'Tis the Art at the Door that will please the best ;
To the end of Time 'twill be still the same,
For the Earth first laughed when the children
   came !

THE DISTRESSED POET.

A SUGGESTION FROM HOGARTH.

ONE knows the scene so well, — a touch,
    A word, brings back again
That room, not garnished overmuch,
    In gusty Drury Lane;

The empty safe, the child that cries,
    The kittens on the coat,
The good-wife with her patient eyes,
    The milkmaid's tuneless throat;

And last, in that mute woe sublime,
    The luckless verseman's air:
The " Bysshe," the foolscap and the rhyme, —
    The Rhyme . . . that is not there!

Poor Bard! to dream the verse inspired —
    With dews Castalian wet —
Is built from cold abstractions squired
    By " Bysshe," his epithet!

Ah ! when she comes, the glad-eyed Muse,
  No step upon the stair
Betrays the guest that none refuse, —
  She takes us unaware ;

And tips with fire our lyric lips,
  And sets our hearts a-flame,
And then, like Ariel, off she trips,
  And none know how she came.

Only, henceforth, for right or wrong,
  By some dull sense grown keen,
Some blank hour blossomed into song,
  We feel that she has been.

JOCOSA LYRA.

I N our hearts is the Great One of Avon
    Engraven,
And we climb the cold summits once built on
    By Milton.

But at times not the air that is rarest
    Is fairest,
And we long in the valley to follow
    Apollo.

Then we drop from the heights atmospheric
    To Herrick,
Or we pour the Greek honey, grown blander,
    Of Landor ;

Or our cosiest nook in the shade is
    Where Praed is,
Or we toss the light bells of the mocker
    With Locker.

Oh, the song where not one of the Graces
    Tight-laces, —

Where we woo the sweet Muses not starchly,
     But archly, —

Where the verse, like a piper a-Maying,
      Comes playing, —
And the rhyme is as gay as a dancer
      In answer, —

It will last till men weary of pleasure
      In measure !
It will last till men weary of laughter . . .
      And after !

MY BOOKS.

THEY dwell in the odour of camphor,
    They stand in a Sheraton shrine,
They are " warranted early editions,"
    These worshipful tomes of mine ; —

In their creamiest " Oxford vellum,"
    In their redolent " crushed Levant,"
With their delicate watered linings,
    They are jewels of price, I grant ; —

Blind-tooled and morocco-jointed,
    They have Zaehnsdorf's daintiest dress,
They are graceful, attenuate, polished,
    But they gather the dust, no less ; —

For the row that I prize is yonder,
    Away on the unglazed shelves,
The bulged and the bruised *octavos*,
    The dear and the dumpy twelves, —

Montaigne with his sheepskin blistered,
    And Howell the worse for wear,

And the worm-drilled Jesuits' Horace,
  And the little old cropped Molière,

And the Burton I bought for a florin,
  And the Rabelais foxed and flea'd, —
For the others I never have opened,
  But those are the books I read.

THE BOOK–PLATE'S PETITION.

BY A GENTLEMAN OF THE TEMPLE.

WHILE cynic CHARLES still trimm'd the vane
　　'Twixt *Querouaille* and *Castlemaine*,
In days that shocked JOHN EVELYN,
My First Possessor fixed me in.
In days of *Dutchmen* and of frost,
The narrow sea with JAMES I cross'd,
Returning when once more began
The Age of *Saturn* and of ANNE.
I am a part of all the past ;
I knew the GEORGES, first and last ;
I have been oft where else was none
Save the great wig of ADDISON ;
And seen on shelves beneath me grope
The little eager form of POPE.
I lost the Third that owned me when
French NOAILLES fled at Dettingen ;
The year JAMES WOLFE surpris'd Quebec,
The Fourth in hunting broke his neck ;
The day that WILLIAM HOGARTH dy'd,
The Fifth one found me in Cheapside.
This was a *Scholar*, one of those
Whose *Greek* is sounder than their *hose ;*

He lov'd old Books and nappy ale,
So liv'd at Streatham, next to THRALE.
'Twas there this stain of grease I boast
Was made by Dr. JOHNSON's toast.
(He did it, as I think, for Spite;
My Master call'd him *Jacobite !*)
And now that I so long to-day
Have rested *post discrimina,*
Safe in the brass-wir'd book-case where
I watch'd the Vicar's whit'ning hair,
Must I these travell'd bones inter
In some *Collector's* sepulchre !
Must I be torn from hence and thrown
With *frontispiece* and *colophon !*
With vagrant *E's*, and *I's*, and *O's*,
The spoil of plunder'd *Folios !*
With scraps and snippets that to ME
Are naught but *kitchen company !*
Nay, rather, FRIEND, this favour grant me :
Tear me at once ; *but don't transplant me.*

CHELTENHAM,
Sept. 31, 1792.

PALOMYDES.

HIM best in all the dim Arthuriad,
  Of lovers of fair women, him I prize, —
The Pagan Palomydes. Never glad
  Was he with sweetness of his lady's eyes,
    Nor joy he had.

But, unloved ever, still must love the same,
  And riding ever through a lonely world,
Whene'er on adverse shield or crest he came,
  Against the danger desperately hurled,
    Crying her name.

So I, who strove to You I may not earn,
  Methinks, am come unto so high a place,
That though from hence I can but vainly yearn
  For that averted favour of your face,
    I shall not turn.

No, I am come too high. Whate'er betide,
  To find the doubtful thing that fights with me,
Toward the mountain tops I still shall ride,
  And cry your name in my extremity,
    As Palomyde,

Until the issue come.   Will it disclose
 No gift of grace, no pity made complete,
After much labour done, — much war with woes?
 Will you deny me still in Heaven, my sweet; —
  Ah, Death — who knows?

ANDRÉ LE CHAPELAIN.

(*Clerk of Love*, 1170.)

HIS PLAINT TO VENUS OF THE COMING YEARS.

"*Plus ne suis ce que j'ay esté*
Et ne le sçaurois jamais estre ;
Mon beau printemps et mon esté
Ont fait le saut par la fenestre."
CLEMENT MAROT, 1537.

QUEEN VENUS, round whose feet,
    To tend thy sacred fire,
With service bitter-sweet
    Nor youths nor maidens tire ; —
Goddess, whose bounties be
Large as the un-oared sea ; —

Mother, whose eldest born
    First stirred his stammering tongue,
In the world's youngest morn,
    When the first daisies sprung : —
Whose last, when Time shall die,
In the same grave shall lie : —

91

Hear thou one suppliant more !
  Must I, thy Bard, grow old,
Bent, with the temples frore,
  Not jocund be nor bold,
To tune for folk in May
Ballad and virelay ?

Shall the youths jeer and jape,
  " Behold his verse doth dote, —
Leave thou Love's lute to scrape,
  And tune thy wrinkled throat
To songs of ' Flesh is Grass,' " —
Shall they cry thus and pass ?

And the sweet girls go by ?
  " Beshrew the grey-beard's tune ! —
What ails his minstrelsy
  To sing us snow in June ! "
Shall they too laugh, and fleet
Far in the sun-warmed street ?

But Thou, whose beauty bright,
  Upon thy wooded hill,
With ineffectual light
  The wan sun seeketh still ; —
Woman, whose tears are dried,
Hardly, for Adon's side, —

Have pity, Erycine !
  Withhold not all thy sweets ;
Must I thy gifts resign
  For Love's mere broken meats ;
And suit for alms prefer
That was thine Almoner ?

Must I, as bondsman, kneel
  That, in full many a cause,
Have scrolled thy just appeal ?
  Have I not writ thy Laws ?
That none from Love shall take
Save but for Love's sweet sake ; —

That none shall aught refuse
To Love of Love's fair dues ; —
That none dear Love shall scoff
Or deem foul shame thereof ; —
That none shall traitor be
To Love's own secrecy ; —

Avert, — avert it, Queen !
  Debarred thy listed sports,
Let me at least be seen
  An usher in thy courts,
Outworn, but still indued
With badge of servitude.

93

When I no more may go,
　As one who treads on air,
To string-notes soft and slow,
　By maids found sweet and fair —
When I no more may be
Of Love's blithe company ; —

When I no more may sit
　Within thine own pleasànce,
To weave, in sentence fit,
　Thy golden dalliance ;
When other hands than these
Record thy soft decrees ; —

Leave me at least to sing
　About thine outer wall,
To tell thy pleasuring,
　Thy mirth, thy festival ;
Yea, let my swan-song be
Thy grace, thy sanctity.

[*Here ended André's words :
　But One that writeth, saith —
Betwixt his stricken chords
　He heard the Wheels of Death ;
And knew the fruits Love bare
But Dead-Sea apples were.*]

THE WATER OF GOLD.

" BUY,—who'll buy?" In the market-place,
    Out of the market din and clatter,
The quack with his puckered persuasive face
    Patters away in the ancient patter.

" Buy, — who'll buy? In this flask I hold —
    In this little flask that I tap with my stick, sir—
Is the famed, infallible Water of Gold, —
    The One, Original, True Elixir !

"Buy—who'll buy? There's a maiden there,—
    She with the ell-long flaxen tresses, —
Here is a draught that will make you fair,
    Fit for an emperor's own caresses !

" Buy, — who'll buy? Are you old and gray?
    Drink but of this, and in less than a minute,
Lo ! you will dance like the flowers in May,
    Chirp and chirk like a new-fledged linnet !

" Buy, — who'll buy? Is a baby ill?
    Drop but a drop of this in his throttle,

Straight he will gossip and gorge his fill,
  Brisk as a burgher over a bottle !

" Here is wealth for your life, — if you will but
      ask ;
  Here is health for your limb, without lint or
      lotion ;
Here is all that you lack, in this tiny flask ;
  And the price is a couple of silver groschen !

" Buy, — who 'll buy ?"   So the tale runs on :
  And still in the great world's market-places
The Quack, with his quack catholicon,
  Finds ever his crowd of upturned faces ;

For he plays on our hearts with his pipe and drum,
  On our vague regret, on our weary yearning ;
For he sells the thing that never can come,
  Or the thing that has vanished, past returning.

A FANCY FROM FONTENELLE.

"De mémoires de Roses on n'a point vu mourir le Jardinier."

THE Rose in the garden slipped her bud,
    And she laughed in the pride of her youthful
        blood,
As she thought of the Gardener standing by —
" He is old, — so old ! And he soon must die ! "

The full Rose waxed in the warm June air,
And she spread and spread till her heart lay bare ;
And she laughed once more as she heard his
        tread —
" He is older now ! He will soon be dead ! "

But the breeze of the morning blew, and found
That the leaves of the blown Rose strewed the
        ground ;
And he came at noon, that Gardener old,
And he raked them gently under the mould.

And I wove the thing to a random rhyme,
For the Rose is Beauty, the Gardener, Time.

DON QUIXOTE.

BEHIND thy pasteboard, on thy battered hack,
    Thy lean cheek striped with plaster to and
        fro,
Thy long spear levelled at the unseen foe,
And doubtful Sancho trudging at thy back,
Thou wert a figure strange enough, good lack !
To make Wiseacredom, both high and low,
Rub purblind eyes, and (having watched thee go)
Dispatch its Dogberrys upon thy track :
Alas ! poor Knight !   Alas ! poor soul possest !
Yet would to-day when Courtesy grows chill,
And life's fine loyalties are turned to jest,
Some fire of thine might burn within us still !
Ah, would but one might lay his lance in rest,
And charge in earnest — were it but a mill !

A BROKEN SWORD.

(To A. L.)

THE shopman shambled from the doorway out
   And twitched it down —
Snapped in the blade !   'Twas scarcely dear, I
  doubt,
   At half-a-crown.

Useless enough !   And yet can still be seen,
   In letters clear,
Traced on the metal's rusty damaskeen —
   "*Povr Paruenyr.*"

Whose was it once ?—Who manned it once in hope
   His fate to gain ?
Who was it dreamed his oyster-world should ope
   To this — in vain ?

Maybe with some stout Argonaut it sailed
   The Western Seas ;
Maybe but to some paltry Nym availed
   For toasting cheese !

Or decked by Beauty on some morning lawn
       With silken knot,
Perchance, ere night, for Church and King 'twas
      drawn —
        Perchance 'twas not !

Who knows — or cares ? To-day, 'mid foils and
      gloves
        Its hilt depends,
Flanked by the favours of forgotten loves, —
        Remembered friends ; —

And oft its legend lends, in hours of stress,
        A word to aid ;
Or like a warning comes, in puffed success,
        Its broken blade.

THE POET'S SEAT.

AN IDYLL OF THE SUBURBS.

" *Ille terrarum mihi præter omnes*
Angulus Ridet."
— Hor. ii. 6.

I T was an elm-tree root of yore,
  With lordly trunk, before they lopped it,
And weighty, said those five who bore
  Its bulk across the lawn, and dropped it
Not once or twice, before it lay,
  With two young pear-trees to protect it,
Safe where the Poet hoped some day
  The curious pilgrim would inspect it.

He saw him with his Poet's eye,
  The tall Maori, turned from etching
The ruin of St. Paul's, to try
  Some object better worth the sketching : —
He saw him, and it nerved his strength
  What time he hacked and hewed and scraped it,
Until the monster grew at length
  The Master-piece to which he shaped it.

101

To wit — a goodly garden seat,
   And fit alike for Shah or Sophy,
With shelf for cigarettes complete,
   And one, but lower down, for coffee ;
He planted pansies 'round its foot, —
   " Pansies for thoughts ! " and rose and arum ;
The Motto (that he meant to put)
   Was " *Ille angulus terrarum.*"

But " Oh ! the change " (as Milton sings) —
   " The heavy change ! " When May departed,
When June with its " delightful things "
   Had come and gone, the rough bark started, —
Began to lose its sylvan brown,
   Grew parched, and powdery, and spotted ;
And, though the Poet nailed it down,
   It still flapped up, and dropped, and rotted.

Nor was this all. 'Twas next the scene
   Of vague (and viscous) vegetations ;
Queer fissures gaped, with oozings green,
   And moist, unsavoury exhalations, —
Faint wafts of wood decayed and sick,
   Till, where he meant to carve his Motto,
Strange leathery fungi sprouted thick,
   And made it like an oyster grotto.

Briefly, it grew a seat of scorn,
   Bare, — shameless, — till, for fresh disaster,
From end to end, one April morn,
   'Twas riddled like a pepper caster, —
Drilled like a vellum of old time ;
   And musing on this final mystery,
The Poet left off scribbling rhyme,
   And took to studying Natural History.

This was the turning of the tide ;
   His five-act play is still unwritten ;
The dreams that now his soul divide
   Are more of Lubbock than of Lytton ;
" *Ballades* " are " verses vain " to him
   Whose first ambition is to lecture
(So much is man the sport of whim !)
   On " Insects and their Architecture."

THE LOST ELIXIR.

" One drop of ruddy human blood puts more life into the
veins of a poem than all the delusive 'aurum potabile' that
can be distilled out of the choicest library." — LOWELL.

A H, yes, that " drop of human blood ! " —
    We had it once, may be,
When our young song's impetuous flood
    First poured its ecstasy ;
But now the shrunk poetic vein
Yields not that priceless drop again.

We toil, — as toiled we not of old ;
    Our patient hands distil
The shining spheres of chemic gold
    With hard-won, fruitless skill ;
But that red drop still seems to be
Beyond our utmost alchemy.

Perchance, but most in later age,
    Time's after-gift, a tear,
Will strike a pathos on the page
    Beyond all art sincere ;
But that " one drop of human blood "
Has gone with life's first leaf and bud.

MEMORIAL VERSES.

A DIALOGUE

TO THE MEMORY OF MR. ALEXANDER POPE.

" Non injussa cano."
VIRG.

POET. I sing of POPE —

FRIEND. What, POPE, the *Twitnam* Bard,
Whom *Dennis, Cibber, Tibbald* push'd so hard !
POPE of the *Dunciad !* POPE who dar'd to woo,
And then to libel, *Wortley-Montagu !*
POPE of the *Ham-walks* story —

                        P. Scandals all !
Scandals that now I care not to recall.
Surely a little, in two hundred Years,
One may neglect Contemporary Sneers : —
Surely Allowance for the Man may make
That had all *Grub-street* yelping in his Wake !
And who (I ask you) has been never Mean,
When urged by Envy, Anger or the Spleen ?
No : I prefer to look on POPE as one
Not rightly happy till his Life was done ;

Whose whole Career, romance it as you please,
Was (what he call'd it) but a " long Disease : "
Think of his Lot, — his Pilgrimage of Pain,
His " crazy Carcass " and his restless Brain ;
Think of his Night-Hours with their Feet of Lead,
His dreary Vigil and his aching Head ;
Think of all this, and marvel then to find
The " crooked Body with a crooked Mind ! "
Nay rather, marvel that, in Fate's Despite,
You find so much to solace and delight, —
So much of Courage, and of Purpose high
In that unequal Struggle *not* to die.
I grant you freely that Pope played his Part
Sometimes ignobly — but he lov'd his Art ;
I grant you freely that he sought his Ends
Not always wisely — but he lov'd his Friends ;
And who of Friends a nobler Roll could show —
Swift, St. John, Bathurst, Marchmont, Peterb'ro',
Arbuthnot —

           Fr. Atticus ?

                  P. Well (*entre nous*),
Most that he said of *Addison* was *true.*
Plain Truth, you know —

               Fr.   Is often not polite
(So *Hamlet* thought) —

P.   And *Hamlet* (Sir) was right.
But leave POPE's Life. To-day, methinks, we touch
The Work too little and the Man too much.
Take up the *Lock*, the *Satires*, *Eloise* —
What Art supreme, what Elegance, what Ease !
How keen the Irony, the Wit how bright,
The Style how rapid, and the Verse how light !
Then read once more, and you shall wonder yet
At Skill, at Turn, at Point, at Epithet.
" True Wit is Nature to Advantage dress'd " —
Was ever Thought so pithily express'd ?
"And ten low Words oft creep in one dull Line "—
Ah, what a Homily on Yours . . and Mine !
Or take — to choose at Random — take but This —
" Ten censure wrong for one that writes amiss."

FR.   Pack'd and precise, no Doubt.   Yet
    surely those
Are but the Qualities we ask of Prose.
Was he a POET ?

P.   Yes : if that be what
Byron was certainly and *Bowles* was not ;
Or say you grant him, to come nearer Date,
What *Dryden* had, that was denied to *Tate* —

FR.   Which means, you claim for him the Spark
    divine,
Yet scarce would place him on the highest Line —

P. True, there are Classes. Pope was most
of all
Akin to *Horace, Persius, Juvenal;*
Pope was, like them, the Censor of his Age,
An Age more suited to Repose than Rage;
When Rhyming turn'd from Freedom to the
Schools,
And shock'd with Licence, shudder'd into Rules;
When *Phœbus* touch'd the Poet's trembling Ear
With one supreme Commandment *Be thou Clear;*
When Thought meant less to reason than compile,
And the *Muse* labour'd .. chiefly with the File.
Beneath full Wigs no Lyric drew its Breath
As in the Days of great Elizabeth;
And to the Bards of Anna was denied
The Note that *Wordsworth* heard on *Duddon*-side.
But Pope took up his Parable, and knit
The Woof of Wisdom with the Warp of Wit;
He trimm'd the Measure on its equal Feet,
And smooth'd and fitted till the Line was neat;
He taught the Pause with due Effect to fall;
He taught the Epigram to come at Call;
He wrote —

Fr. His *Iliad!*

P. Well, suppose you own
You like your *Iliad* in the Prose of *Bohn,* —

Tho' if you'd learn in Prose how *Homer* sang,
'Twere best to learn of *Butcher* and of *Lang*, —
Suppose you say your Worst of POPE, declare
His Jewels Paste, his Nature a Parterre,
His Art but Artifice — I ask once more
Where have you seen such Artifice before ?
Where have you seen a Parterre better grac'd,
Or gems that glitter like his Gems of Paste ?
Where can you show, among your Names of
Note,
So much to copy and so much to quote ?
And where, in Fine, in all our English Verse,
A Style more trenchant and a Sense more terse ?

So I, that love the old *Augustan* Days
Of formal Courtesies and formal Phrase ;
That like along the finish'd Line to feel
The Ruffle's Flutter and the Flash of Steel ;
That like my Couplet as compact as clear ;
That like my Satire sparkling tho' severe,
Unmix'd with Bathos and unmarr'd by Trope,
I fling my Cap for Polish — and for POPE !

A FAMILIAR EPISTLE

*To * * Esq. of * * with a Life of the late Ingenious*
Mr. Wm. Hogarth.

DEAR Cosmopolitan, — I know
    I should address you a *Rondeau,*
Or else announce what I 've to say
At least *en Ballade fratrisée;*
But No : for once I leave Gymnasticks,
And take to simple *Hudibrasticks;*
Why should I choose another Way,
When this was good enough for GAY?

    You love, my FRIEND, with me, I think,
That Age of Lustre and of Link ;
Of *Chelsea* China and long "s"es,
Of Bag-wigs and of flowered Dresses ;
That Age of Folly and of Cards,
Of Hackney Chairs and Hackney Bards ;
—No H—LTS, no K—G—N P—LS were then
Dispensing Competence to Men ;
The gentle Trade was left to Churls,
Your frowsy TONSONS and your CURLLS :

Mere Wolves in Ambush to attack
The AUTHOR in a Sheep-skin Back ;
Then SAVAGE and his Brother-Sinners
In *Porridge-Island* div'd for Dinners ;
Or doz'd on *Covent Garden* Bulks,
And liken'd Letters to the Hulks ; —
You know that by-gone Time, I say,
That aimless easy-moral'd Day,
When rosy Morn found MADAM still
Wrangling at *Ombre* or *Quadrille,*
When good Sir JOHN reel'd Home to Bed,
From *Pontack's* or the *Shakespear's Head ;*
When TRIP *convey'd* his Master's Cloaths,
And took his Titles and his Oaths ;
While BETTY, in a cast *Brocade,*
Ogled MY LORD at Masquerade ;
When GARRICK play'd the guilty *Richard,*
Or mouth'd *Macbeth* with Mrs. PRITCHARD ;
When FOOTE grimac'd his snarling Wit ;
When CHURCHILL bullied in the Pit ;
When the CUZZONI sang —

> But there !

The further Catalogue I spare,
Having no Purpose to eclipse
That tedious Tale of HOMER's Ships ; —
This is the MAN that drew it all
From *Pannier Alley* to the *Mall,*

Then turn'd and drew it once again
From *Bird-Cage Walk* to *Lewknor's Lane;* —
Its Rakes and Fools, its Rogues and Sots;
Its brawling Quacks, its starveling Scots;
Its Ups and Downs, its Rags and Garters,
Its HENLEYS, LOVATS, MALCOLMS, CHARTRES;
Its Splendour, Squalor, Shame, Disease;
Its *quicquid agunt Homines;* —
Nor yet omitted to pourtray
Furens quid possit Foemina; —
In short, held up to ev'ry Class
NATURE'S unflatt'ring looking-Glass;
And, from his Canvass, spoke to All
The Message of a JUVENAL.

Take Him.   His Merits most aver:
His weak Point is — his Chronicler!

NOV^R. 1, 1879.

HENRY FIELDING.

(To James Russell Lowell.)

NOT from the ranks of those we call
    Philosopher or Admiral, —
Neither as LOCKE was, nor as BLAKE,
Is that Great Genius for whose sake
We keep this Autumn festival.

And yet in one sense, too, was he
A soldier — of humanity ;
And, surely, philosophic mind
Belonged to him whose brain designed
That teeming COMIC EPOS where,
As in CERVANTES and MOLIÈRE,
Jostles the medley of Mankind.

Our ENGLISH NOVEL'S pioneer !
His was the eye that first saw clear
How, not in natures half-effaced
By cant of Fashion and of Taste, —
Not in the circles of the Great,
Faint-blooded and exanimate, —

Lay the true field of Jest and Whim,
Which we to-day reap after him.
No : — he stepped lower down and took
The piebald PEOPLE for his Book !

Ah, what a wealth of Life there is
In that large-laughing page of his !
What store and stock of Common-Sense,
Wit, Wisdom, Books, Experience !
How his keen Satire flashes through,
And cuts a sophistry in two !
How his ironic lightning plays
Around a rogue and all his ways !
Ah, how he knots his lash to see
That ancient cloak, Hypocrisy !

Whose are the characters that give
Such round reality ? — that live
With such full pulse ?   Fair SOPHY yet
Sings *Bobbing Joan* at the spinet ;
We see AMELIA cooking still
That supper for the recreant WILL ;
We hear Squire WESTERN's headlong tones
Bawling " Wut ha ? — wut ha ? " to JONES.
Are they not present now to us, —
The Parson with his *Æschylus ?*
SLIPSLOP the frail, and NORTHERTON,

PARTRIDGE, and BATH, and HARRISON ? —
Are they not breathing, moving, — all
The motley, merry carnival
That FIELDING kept, in days agone ?

He was the first who dared to draw
Mankind the mixture that he saw ;   ·
Not wholly good nor ill, but both,
With fine intricacies of growth.
He pulled the wraps of flesh apart,
And showed the working human heart ;
He scorned to drape the truthful nude
With smooth, decorous platitude !

He was too frank, may be ; and dared
Too boldly.   Those whose faults he bared,
Writhed in the ruthless grasp that brought
Into the light their secret thought.
Therefore the TARTUFFE-throng who say
'' *Couvrez ce sein,*'' and look that way, —
Therefore the Priests of Sentiment
Rose on him with their garments rent.
Therefore the gadfly swarm whose sting
Plies ever round some generous thing,
Buzzed of old bills and tavern-scores,
Old '' might-have-beens '' and '' heretofores '' ; —
Then, from that garbled record-list,
Made him his own Apologist.

And was he ?   Nay, — let who has known
Nor Youth nor Error, cast the stone !
If to have sense of Joy and Pain
Too keen, — to rise, to fall again,
To live too much, — be sin, why then,
This was no pattern among men.
But those who turn that later page,
The Journal of his middle-age,
Watch him serene in either fate, —
Philanthropist and Magistrate ;
Watch him as Husband, Father, Friend,
Faithful, and patient to the end ;
Grieving, as e'en the brave may grieve,
But for the loved ones he must leave :
These will admit — if any can —
That 'neath the green Estrella trees,
No Artist merely, but a MAN,
Wrought on our noblest island-plan,
Sleeps with the alien Portuguese.

HENRY WADSWORTH LONGFELLOW.

" Nec turpem senectam
Degere, nec cithara carentem."
— HOR. i. 31.

" NOT to be tuneless in old age ! "
   Ah ! surely blest his pilgrimage,
Who, in his Winter's snow,
Still sings with note as sweet and clear
As in the morning of the year
   When the first violets blow !

Blest ! — but more blest, whom Summer's heat,
Whom Spring's impulsive stir and beat,
   Have taught no feverish lure ;
Whose Muse, benignant and serene,
Still keeps his Autumn chaplet green
   Because his verse is pure !

Lie calm, O white and laureate head !
Lie calm, O Dead, that art not dead,
   Since from the voiceless grave,
Thy voice shall speak to old and young
While song yet speaks an English tongue
   By Charles' or Thamis' wave !

119

CHARLES GEORGE GORDON.

" RATHER be dead than praised," he said,
    That hero, like a hero dead,
In this slack-sinewed age endued
With more than antique fortitude !

" Rather be dead than praised ! " Shall we,
Who loved thee, now that Death sets free
Thine eager soul, with word and line
Profane that empty house of thine ?

Nay, — let us hold, be mute. Our pain
Will not be less that we refrain ;
And this our silence shall but be
A larger monument to thee.

VICTOR HUGO.

H E set the trumpet to his lips, and lo !
 The clash of waves, the roar of winds that
 blow,
The strife and stress of Nature's warring things,
Rose like a storm-cloud, upon angry wings.

He set the reed-pipe to his lips, and lo !
The wreck of landscape took a rosy glow,
And Life, and Love, and gladness that Love brings
Laughed in the music, like a child that sings.

Master of each, Arch-Master ! We that still
Wait in the verge and outskirt of the Hill
Look upward lonely — lonely to the height
Where thou has climbed, for ever, out of sight !

ALFRED, LORD TENNYSON.

EMIGRAVIT, OCTOBER VI., MDCCCXCII.

GRIEF there will be, and may,
 When King Apollo's bay
Is cut midwise ;
Grief that a song is stilled,
Grief for the unfulfilled
Singer that dies.

Not so we mourn thee now,
Not so we grieve that thou,
MASTER, art passed,
Since thou thy song didst raise,
Through the full round of days,
E'en to the last.

Grief there may be, and will,
When that the Singer still
Sinks in the song ;
When that the wingéd rhyme
Fails of the promised prime,
Ruined and wrong.

Not thus we mourn thee — we —
Not thus we grieve for thee,
MASTER and Friend ;
Since, like a clearing flame,
Clearer thy pure song came
E'en to the end.

Nay — nor for thee we grieve
E'en as for those that leave
Life without name ;
Lost as the stars that set,
Empty of men's regret,
Empty of fame.

Rather we count thee one
Who, when his race is run,
Layeth him down,
Calm — through all coming days,
Filled with a nation's praise,
Filled with renown.

FABLES OF LITERATURE AND ART.

125

THE POET AND THE CRITICS.

I F those who wield the Rod forget,
  'Tis truly — *Quis custodiet ?*

A certain Bard (as Bards will do)
Dressed up his Poems for Review.
His Type was plain, his Title clear ;
His Frontispiece by FOURDRINIER.
Moreover, he had on the Back
A sort of sheepskin Zodiac ; —
A Mask, a Harp, an Owl, — in fine,
A neat and " classical " Design.
But the *in*-Side ? — Well, good or bad,
The Inside was the best he had :
Much Memory, — more Imitation ; —
Some Accidents of Inspiration ; —
Some Essays in that finer Fashion
Where Fancy takes the place of Passion ; —
And some (of course) more roughly wrought
To catch the Advocates of Thought. ·

In the less-crowded Age of ANNE,
Our Bard had been a favoured Man ;

Fortune, more chary with the Sickle,
Had ranked him next to GARTH or TICKELL ; —
He might have even dared to hope
A Line's Malignity from POPE !
But now, when Folks are hard to please,
And Poets are as thick as — Peas,
The Fates are not so prone to flatter,
Unless, indeed, a Friend . . . . No Matter.

The Book, then, had a minor Credit :
The Critics took, and doubtless read it.
Said A. — *These little Songs display*
No lyric Gift; but still a Ray, —
A Promise.   They will do ño Harm.
'Twas kindly, if not *very* warm.
Said B. — *The Author may, in time,*
Acquire the Rudiments of Rhyme :
His Efforts now are scarcely Verse.
This, certainly, could not be worse.

Sorely discomfited, our Bard
Worked for another ten Years — hard.
Meanwhile the World, unmoved, went on ;
New Stars shot up, shone out, were gone ;
Before his second Volume came
His Critics had forgot his Name :

And who, forsooth, is bound to know
Each Laureate *in embryo !*
They tried and tested him, no less,—
The sworn Assayers of the Press.
Said A. — *The Author may, in Time* . . . .
Or much what B. had said of Rhyme.
Then B. — *These little Songs display* . . . .
And so forth, in the sense of A.
Over the Bard I throw a Veil.

There is no MORAL to this Tale.

THE TOYMAN.

WITH Verse, is Form the first, or Sense?
    Hereon men waste their Eloquence.

"Sense (cry the one Side), Sense, of course.
How can you lend your Theme its Force?
How can you be direct and clear,
Concise, and (best of all) sincere,
If you must pen your Strain sublime
In Bonds of Measure and of Rhyme?
Who ever heard true Grief relate
Its heartfelt Woes in 'six' and 'eight'?
Or felt his manly Bosom swell
Beneath a French-made *Villanelle?*
How can your *Mens divinior* sing
Within the Sonnet's scanty Ring,
Where she must chant her Orphic Tale
In just so many Lines, or fail? . . ."

" Form is the first (the Others bawl);
If not, why write in Verse at all?
Why not your throbbing Thoughts expose
(If verse be such Restraint) in Prose?

For surely if you speak your Soul
Most freely where there's least Control,
It follows you must speak it best
By Rhyme (or Reason) unreprest.
Blest Hour! be not delayed too long,
When Britain frees her Slaves of Song;
And barred no more by Lack of Skill,
The Mob may crowd *Parnassus* Hill ! . . "

Just at this Point — for you must know,
All this was but the To-and-fro
Of MATT and DICK who played with Thought,
And lingered longer than they ought
(So pleasant 'tis to tap one's Box
And trifle round a Paradox !) —
There came — but I forgot to say,
'Twas in the Mall, the Month was May —
There came a Fellow where they sat,
His Elf-locks peeping through his Hat,
Who bore a Basket.   Straight his Load
He set upon the Ground, and showed
His newest Toy — a Card with Strings.
On this side was a Bird with Wings,
On that, a Cage.   You twirled, and lo !
The Twain were one.

     Said MATT, " E'en so.

Here's the Solution in a Word : —
Form is the Cage and Sense the Bird.
The Poet twirls them in his Mind,
And wins the Trick with both combined."

.

THE SUCCESSFUL AUTHOR.

WHEN Fate presents us with the Bays,
　　We prize the Praiser, not the Praise.
We scarcely think our Fame eternal
If vouched for by the *Farthing Journal;*
But when the *Craftsman's* self has spoken,
We take it for a certain Token.
This an Example best will show,
Derived from DENNIS DIDEROT.

A hackney Author, who'd essayed
All Hazards of the scribbling Trade ;
And failed to live by every Mode,
From *Persian Tale* to *Birthday Ode;*
Embarked at last, thro' pure Starvation,
In Theologic Speculation.
'Tis commonly affirmed his Pen
Had been most orthodox till then ;
But oft, as SOCRATES has said,
The Stomach's stronger than the Head ;
And, for a sudden Change of Creed,
There is no *Jesuit* like Need.
Then, too, 'twas cheap ; he took it all,

By force of Habit, from the Gaul.
He showed (the Trick is nowise new)
That Nothing we believe is true ;
But chiefly that Mistake is rife
Touching the point of *After-Life ;*
Here all were wrong from PLATO down :
His Price (in Boards) was Half-a-Crown.
The Thing created quite a Scare : —
He got a Letter from VOLTAIRE,
Naming him *Ami* and *Confrère ;*
Besides two most attractive Offers
Of Chaplaincies from noted Scoffers.
He fell forthwith his Head to lift,
To talk of " I and DR. SW—FT ; "
And brag, at Clubs, as one who spoke,
On equal Terms, with BOLINGBROKE.
But, at the last, a Missive came
That put the Copestone to his Fame.
The Boy who brought it would not wait :
It bore a *Covent-Garden* Date ; —
A woful Sheet with doubtful Ink,
And Air of *Bridewell* or the *Clink.*
It ran in this wise : — *Learned Sir !*
We, whose Subscriptions follow here,
Desire to state our Fellow-feeling
In this Religion you're revealing.
You make it plain that if so be

We 'scape on Earth from Tyburn Tree,
There's nothing left for us to fear
In this — or any other Sphere.
We offer you our Thanks; and hope
Your Honor, too, may cheat the Rope!
With that came all the Names beneath,
As BLUESKIN, JERRY CLINCH, MACHEATH,
BET CARELESS, and the Rest — a Score
Of Rogues and *Bona Robas* more.

This *Newgate Calendar* he read :
'Tis not recorded what he said.

THE DILETTANT.

THE most oppressive Form of Cant
 Is that of your Art-Dilettant : —
Or rather " was." The Race, I own,
To-day is, happily, unknown.

A Painter, now by Fame forgot,
Had painted — 'tis no matter what ;
Enough that he resolved to try
The Verdict of a critic Eye.
The Friend he sought made no Pretence
To more than candid Common-sense,
Nor held himself from Fault exempt.
He praised, it seems, the whole Attempt.
Then, pausing long, showed here and there
That Parts required a nicer Care, —
A closer Thought. The Artist heard,
Expostulated, chafed, demurred.

Just then popped in a passing Beau,
Half Pertness, half Pulvilio ; —
One of those Mushroom Growths that spring
From *Grand Tours* and from Tailoring ; —
And dealing much in terms of Art

Picked up at Sale and auction Mart.
Straight to the Masterpiece he ran
With lifted Glass, and thus began,
Mumbling as fast as he could speak : —
" Sublime ! — prodigious ! — truly Greek !
That 'Air of Head' is just divine ;
That contour GUIDO, every line ;
That Forearm, too, has quite the *Gusto*
Of the third Manner of ROBUSTO . . . ."
Then, with a Simper and a Cough,
He skipped a little farther off : —
" The middle Distance, too, is placed
Quite in the best Italian Taste ;
And Nothing could be more effective
Than the *Ordonnance* and Perspective . . . .
You've sold it ? — No ? — Then take my word,
I shall speak of it to MY LORD.
What ! — I insist.   Don't stir, I beg.
Adieu ! "   With that he made a Leg,
Offered on either Side his Box, —
So took his *Virtù* off to COCK'S.

The Critic, with a Shrug, once more
Turned to the Canvas as before.
" Nay," — said the Painter — " I allow
The Worst that you can tell me now.
'Tis plain my Art must go to School,
To win such Praises — from a FOOL ! "

THE TWO PAINTERS.

I N Art some hold Themselves content
  If they but compass what they meant ;
Others prefer, their Purpose gained,
Still to find Something unattained —
Something whereto they vaguely grope
With no more Aid than that of Hope.
Which are the Wiser ? Who shall say !
The prudent Follower of GAY
Declines to speak for either View,
But sets his Fable 'twixt the two.

Once — 'twas in good Queen ANNA's Time —
While yet in this benighted Clime
The GENIUS of the ARTS (now known
On mouldy Pediments alone)
Protected all the Men of Mark,
Two Painters met Her in the Park.
Whether She wore the Robe of Air
Portrayed by VERRIO and LAGUERRE ;
Or, like BELINDA, trod this Earth,
Equipped with Hoop of monstrous Girth,
And armed at every Point for Slaughter

With Essences and Orange-water,
I know not : but it seems that then,
After some talk of Brush and Pen, —
Some chat of Art both High and Low,
Of VAN's "Goose-Pie" and KNELLER's "*Mol*,"—
The Lady, as a Goddess should,
Bade Them ask of Her what They would.
"Then, Madam, my request," says BRISK,
Giving his *Ramillie* a whisk,
" Is that your Majesty will crown
My humble Efforts with Renown.
Let me, I beg it — Thanks to You —
Be praised for Everything I do,
Whether I paint a Man of Note,
Or only plan a Petticoat."
"Nay," quoth the other, " I confess "
(This One was plainer in his Dress,
And even poorly clad), " for me,
I scorn Your Popularity.
Why should I care to catch at once
The Point of View of every Dunce ?
Let me do well, indeed, but find
The Fancy first, the Work behind ;
Nor wholly touch the thing I wanted . . . ."
The Goddess both Petitions granted.

Each in his Way, achieved Success ;
But One grew Great. And which One ? Guess.

THE CLAIMS OF THE MUSE.

TOO oft we hide our Frailties' Blame
    Beneath some simple-sounding Name!
So Folks, who in gilt Coaches ride,
Will call Display but *Proper Pride ;*
So Spendthrifts, who their Acres lose,
Curse not their Folly but the *Jews ;*
So *Madam,* when her Roses faint,
Resorts to . . . . anything but *Paint.*

An honest Uncle, who had plied
His Trade of Mercer in *Cheapside,*
Until his Name on '*Change* was found
Good for some Thirty Thousand Pound,
Was burdened with an Heir inclined
To thoughts of quite a different Kind.
His Nephew dreamed of Naught but Verse
From Morn to Night, and, what was worse,
He quitted all at length to follow
That " sneaking, whey-faced God, APOLLO."
In plainer Words, he ran up Bills
At *Child's,* at *Batson's* and at *Will's ;*
Discussed the Claims of rival Bards

At Midnight, — with a Pack of Cards ;
Or made excuse for " t'other Bottle "
Over a point in ARISTOTLE.
This could not last, and like his Betters
He found, too soon, the *Cost* of Letters.
Back to his Uncle's House he flew,
Confessing that he'd not a *Sou.*
'Tis true, his Reasons, if sincere,
Were more poetical than clear :
"'Alas ! " he said, " I name no Names :
The *Muse,* dear Sir, the *Muse* has claims."
His Uncle, who, behind his Till,
Knew less of *Pindus* than *Snow-Hill,*
Looked grave, but thinking (as Men say)
That Youth but once can have its Day,
Equipped anew his *Pride* and *Hope*
To frisk it on *Parnassus* Slope.
In one short Month he sought the Door
More shorn and ragged than before.
This Time he showed but small Contrition,
And gloried in his mean Condition.
" The greatest of our Race," he said,
" Through *Asian* Cities begged his Bread.
The *Muse* — the *Muse* delights to see
Not *Broadcloth* but *Philosophy !*
Who doubts of this her Honour shames,
But (as you know) she has her Claims . . . ."

141

" Friend," quoth his Uncle then, " I doubt
This scurvy Craft that you're about
Will lead your *philosophic* Feet
Either to *Bedlam* or the *Fleet.*
Still, as I would not have you lack,
Go get some *Broadcloth* to your Back,
And — if it please this precious *Muse* —
'Twere well to purchase decent Shoes.
Though harkye, Sir . . . ." The Youth was
    gone,
Before the good Man could go on.

And yet ere long again was seen
That Votary of *Hippocrene.*
As along *Cheap* his Way he took,
His Uncle spied him by a Brook,
Not such as *Nymphs Castalian* pour, —
'Twas but the Kennel, nothing more.
His Plight was plain by every Sign
Of Idiot Smile and Stains of Wine.
He strove to rise, and wagged his Head —
" The *Muse*, dear Sir, the *Muse* — " he said.
" *Muse!* " quoth the Other, in a Fury,
" The *Muse* shan't serve you, I assure ye.
She's just some wanton, idle *Jade*
That makes young Fools forget their Trade, —

Who should be whipped, if I'd my Will,
From *Charing Cross* to *Ludgate Hill*.
She's just . . . ."   But he began to stutter,
So left Sir Graceless in the Gutter.

THE 'SQUIRE AT VAUXHALL.

NOTHING so idle as to waste
   This Life disputing upon *Taste;*
And most — let that sad Truth be written —
In this contentious Land of *Britain*,
Where each one holds " it seems to me "
Equivalent to *Q. E. D.*,
And if you dare to doubt his Word
Proclaims you Blockhead and absurd.
And then, too often, the Debate
Is not 'twixt First and Second-rate,
Some narrow Issue, where a Touch
Of more or less can't matter much,
But, and this makes the Case so sad,
Betwixt undoubted Good and Bad.
Nay, — there are some so strangely wrought, —
So warped and twisted in their Thought, —
That, if the Fact be but confest,
They like the baser Thing the best.
Take BOTTOM, who for one, 'tis clear,
Possessed a " reasonable Ear ; "
He might have had at his Command
The Symphonies of *Fairy-Land;*

Well, our immortal SHAKESPEAR owns
The Oaf preferred the " Tongs and Bones ! "

'Squire HOMESPUN from *Clod-Hall* rode down,
As the Phrase is — " to see the Town ; "
(The Town, in those Days, mostly lay
Betwixt the *Tavern* and the *Play.*)
Like all their Worships the J.P.'s,
He put up at the *Hercules ;*
Then sallied forth on Shanks his Mare,
Rather than jolt it in a Chair, —
A curst, new-fangled *Little-Ease,*
That knocks your Nose against your Knees.
For the good 'Squire was Country-bred,
And had strange Notions in his Head,
Which made him see in every Cur
The starveling Breed of *Hanover ;*
He classed your Kickshaws and *Ragoos*
With Popery and Wooden Shoes ;
Railed at all Foreign Tongues as Lingo,
And sighed o'er *Chaos* Wine for Stingo.

Hence, as he wandered to and fro,
Nothing could please him, high or low.
As *Savages* at *Ships of War*
He looked unawed on *Temple-Bar ;*

Scarce could conceal his Discontent
With *Fish-Street* and the *Monument ;*
And might (except at Feeding-Hour)
Have scorned the Lion in the *Tower,*
But that the Lion's Race was run,
And — for the Moment — there was none.

At length, blind Fate, that drives us all,
Brought him at Even to *Vauxhall,*
What Time the eager Matron jerks
Her slow Spouse to the *Water-Works,*
And the coy Spinster, half-afraid
Consults the *Hermit* in the Shade.
Dazed with the Din and Crowd, the 'Squire
Sank in a Seat before the Choir.
The FAUSTINETTA, fair and showy,
Warbled an Air from *Arsinoë,*
Playing her Bosom and her Eyes
As Swans do when they agonize.
Alas ! to some a Mug of Ale
Is better than an *Orphic Tale !*
The 'Squire grew dull, the 'Squire grew bored ;
His chin dropt down ; he slept ; he snored.
Then, straying thro' the " poppied Reign,"
He dreamed him at *Clod-Hall* again ;
He heard once more the well-known Sounds,
The Crack of Whip, the Cry of Hounds.

He rubbed his Eyes, woke up, and lo !
A Change had come upon the Show.
Where late the Singer stood, a Fellow,
Clad in a Jockey's Coat of Yellow,
Was mimicking a Cock that crew.
Then came the Cry of Hounds anew,
Yoicks ! Stole Away ! and harking back ;
Then Ringwood leading up the Pack.
The 'Squire in Transport slapped his Knee
At this most hugeous Pleasantry.
The sawn Wood followed ; last of all
The Man brought something in a Shawl, —
Something that struggled, scraped, and squeaked
As Porkers do, whose tails are tweaked.
Our honest 'Squire could scarcely sit
So excellent he thought the Wit.
But when *Sir Wag* drew off the Sheath
And showed there was no Pig beneath,
His pent-up Wonder, Pleasure, Awe,
Exploded in a long Guffaw :
And, to his dying Day, he'd swear
That Naught in Town the Bell could bear
From " Jockey wi' the Yellow Coat
That had a Farm-Yard in his Throat ! "

MORAL THE FIRST you may discover :
The 'Squire was like TITANIA's lover ;

He put a squeaking Pig before
The Harmony of CLAYTON's Score.

MORAL THE SECOND — not so clear ;
But still it shall be added here :
He praised the Thing he understood ;
'Twere well if every Critic would.

THE CLIMACTERIC.

W HEN do the reasoning Powers decline ?
  The Ancients said at Forty-Nine.
At Forty-Nine behoves it then
To quit the Inkhorn and the Pen,
Since ARISTOTLE so decreed.
Premising thus, we now proceed.

In that thrice-favoured Northern Land,
Where most the Flowers of Thought expand,
And all things nebulous grow clear,
Through Spectacles and Lager-Beer,
There lived, at *Dumpelsheim* the Lesser,
A certain High-Dutch Herr Professor.
Than GROTIUS more alert and quick,
More logical than BURGERSDYCK,
His Lectures both so much transcended,
That far and wide his Fame extended,
Proclaiming him to every clime
Within a Mile of *Dumpelsheim*.
But chief he taught, by Day and Night,
The Doctrine of the Stagirite,
Proving it fixed beyond Dispute,

149

In Ways that none could well refute ;
For if by Chance 'twas urged that Men
O'er-stepped the Limit now and then,
He'd show unanswerably still
Either that all they did was " Nil,"
Or else 'twas marked by Indication
Of grievous mental Degradation :
Nay — he could even trace, they say,
That Degradation to a Day.

The Years rolled on, and as they flew,
More famed the Herr Professor grew,
His "*Locus* of the Pineal Gland "
(A Masterpiece he long had planned)
Had reached the End of Book Eleven,
And he was nearing Forty-Seven.
Admirers had not long to wait ;
The last Book came at Forty-Eight,
And should have been the Heart and Soul —
The Crown and Summit — of the whole.
But now the oddest Thing ensued ;
'Twas so insufferably crude,
So feeble and so poor, 'twas plain
The Writer's Mind was on the wane.
Nothing could possibly be said ;
E'en Friendship's self must hang the head,
While jealous Rivals, scarce so civil,

Denounced it openly as " Drivel."
Never was such Collapse.   In brief,
The poor Professor died of Grief.

With fitting mortuary Rhyme
They buried him at *Dumpelsheim,*
And as they sorrowing set about
A " Short Memoir," the Truth came out.
He had been older than he knew.
The Parish Clerk had put a " 2 "
In place of " Nought," and made his Date
Of Birth a Brace of Years too late.
When he had written Book the Last,
His true Climacteric had past !

Moral. —To estimate your Worth,
Be certain as to date of Birth.

TALES IN RHYME.

THE VIRGIN WITH THE BELLS.

MUCH strange is true. And yet so much
    Dan Time thereto of doubtful lays
He blurs them both beneath his touch : —

In this our tale his part he plays.
At Florence, so the legend tells,
There stood a church that men would praise

(Even where Art the most excels)
For works of price ; but chief for one
They called the " Virgin with the Bells."

Gracious she was, and featly done,
With crown of gold about the hair,
And robe of blue with stars thereon,

And sceptre in her hand did bear ;
And o'er her, in an almond tree,
Three little golden bells there were,

Writ with Faith, Hope, and Charity.
None knew from whence she came of old,
Nor whose the sculptor's name should be

Of great or small.   But this they told : —
That once from out the blaze of square,
And bickering folk that bought and sold,

More moved no doubt of heat than prayer,
Came to the church an Umbrian,
Lord of much gold and champaign fair,

But, for all this, a hard, haught man.
To whom the priests, in humbleness,
At once to beg for alms began,

Praying him grant of his excess
Such as for poor men's bread might pay,
Or give their saint a gala-dress.

Thereat with scorn he answered — " Nay,
Most Reverend !   Far too well ye know,
By guile and wile, the fox's way

" To swell the Church's overflow.
But ere from me the least carline
Ye win, this summer's sky shall snow ;

" Or, likelier still, your doll's-eyed queen
Shall ring her bells . . . . but not of craft.
By Bacchus ! ye are none too lean

" For fasting folk ! "   With that he laughed,
And so, across the porphyry floor,
His hand upon his dagger-haft,

Strode, and of these was seen no more.
Nor, of a truth, much marvelled they
At those his words, since gear and store

Oft dower shrunk souls.   But, on a day,
While yet again throughout the square,
The buyers in their noisy way,

Chaffered around the basket ware,
It chanced (I but the tale reveal,
Nor true nor false therein declare) —

It chanced that when the priest would kneel
Before the taper's flickering flame,
Sudden a little tremulous peal

From out the Virgin's altar came.
And they that heard must fain recall
The Umbrian, and the words of shame

Spoke in his pride, and therewithal
Came news how, at that very date
And hour of time was fixed his fall,

157

Who, of the Duke, was banned the State,
And all his goods, and lands as well,
To Holy Church were confiscate.

Such is the tale the Frati tell.

A TALE OF POLYPHEME.

"THERE'S nothing new " — Not that I go
 so far
 As he who also said " There's nothing true,"
Since, on the contrary, I hold there are
 Surviving still a verity or two ;
But, as to novelty, in my conviction,
There's nothing new, — especially in fiction.

Hence, at the outset, I make no apology,
 If this *my* story is as old as Time,
Being, indeed, that idyll of mythology, —
 The Cyclops' love, — which, somewhat varied,
 I'm
To tell once more, the adverse Muse permitting,
In easy rhyme, and phrases neatly fitting.

"Once on a time" — there's nothing new, I
 said —
 It may be fifty years ago or more,
Beside a lonely posting-road that led
 Seaward from Town, there used to stand of
 yore,

With low-built bar and old bow-window shady
An ancient Inn, the " Dragon and the Lady."

Say that by chance, wayfaring Reader mine,
    You cast a shoe, and at this dusty Dragon,
Where beast and man were equal on the sign,
    Inquired at once for Blacksmith and for flagon :
The landlord showed you, while you drank your
        hops,
A road-side break beyond the straggling shops.

And so directed, thereupon you led
    Your halting roadster to a kind of pass,
This you descended with a crumbling tread,
    And found the sea beneath you like a glass ;
And soon, beside a building partly walled —
Half hut, half cave — you raised your voice and
        called.

Then a dog growled ; and straightway there began
    Tumult within — for, bleating with affright,
A goat burst out, escaping from the can ;
    And, following close, rose slowly into sight —
Blind of one eye, and black with toil and tan —
An uncouth, limping, heavy-shouldered man.

Part smith, part seaman, and part shepherd too :
   You scarce knew which, as, pausing with the
      pail
Half filled with goat's milk, silently he drew
   An anvil forth, and reaching shoe and nail,
Bared a red forearm, bringing into view
Anchors and hearts in shadowy tattoo.

And then he lit his fire . . . . But I dispense
   Henceforth with you, my Reader, and your
      horse,
As being but a colorable pretence
   To bring an awkward hero in perforce ;
Since this our smith, for reasons never known,
To most society preferred his own.

Women declared that he'd an " Evil Eye," —
   This in a sense was true — he had but one ;
Men, on the other hand, alleged him shy :
   We sometimes say so of the friends we shun ;
But, wrong or right, suffices to affirm it —
The Cyclops lived a veritable hermit, —

Dwelling below the cliff, beside the sea,
   Caved like an ancient British Troglodyte,
Milking his goat at eve, and it may be,
   Spearing the fish along the flats at night,

Until, at last, one April evening mild,
Came to the Inn a Lady and a Child.

The Lady was a nullity; the Child
  One of those bright bewitching little creatures,
Who, if she once but shyly looked and smiled,
  Would soften out the ruggedest of features;
Fragile and slight, — a very fay for size, —
With pale town-cheeks, and "clear germander
    eyes."

Nurses, no doubt, might name her "somewhat
    wild;"
  And pedants, possibly, pronounce her "slow;"
Or corset-makers add, that for a child,
  She needed "cultivation;"—all I know
Is that whene'er she spoke, or laughed, or romped,
    you
Felt in each act the beauty of impromptu.

The Lady was a nullity — a pale,
  Nerveless and pulseless quasi-invalid,
Who, lest the ozone should in aught avail,
  Remained religiously indoors to read;
So that, in wandering at her will, the Child
Did, in reality, run "somewhat wild."

At first but peering at the sanded floor
   And great shark jaw-bone in the cosy bar ;
Then watching idly from the dusky door,
   The noisy advent of a coach or car ;
Then stealing out to wonder at the fate
Of blistered Ajax by the garden gate, —

Some old ship's figure-head — until at last,
   Straying with each excursion more and more,
She reached the limits of the road, and passed,
   Plucking the pansies, downward to the shore,
And so, as you, respected Reader, showed,
Came to the smith's "desirable abode."

There by the cave the occupant she found,
   Weaving a crate ; and, with a gladsome cry,
The dog frisked out, although the Cyclops frowned
   With all the terrors of his single eye ;
Then from a mound came running, too, the goat,
Uttering her plaintive, desultory note.

The Child stood wondering at the silent man,
   Doubtful to go or stay, when presently
She felt a plucking, for the goat began
   To crop the trail of twining briony
She held behind her ; so that, laughing, she
Turned her light steps, retreating, to the sea.

But the goat followed her on eager feet,
   And therewithal an air so grave and mild,
Coupled with such a deprecatory bleat
   Of injured confidence, that soon the Child
Filled the lone shore with louder merriment,
And e'en the Cyclops' heavy brow unbent.

Thus grew acquaintanceship between the pair,
   The girl and goat ; — for thenceforth, day by
      day,
The Child would bring her four-foot friend such
      fare
   As might be gathered on the downward way : —
Foxglove, or broom, and " yellow cytisus,"
Dear to all goats since Greek Theocritus.

But, for the Cyclops, that misogynist
   Having, by stress of circumstances, smiled,
Felt it at least incumbent to resist
   Further encroachment, and as one beguiled
By adverse fortune, with the half-door shut,
Dwelt in the dim seclusion of his hut.

And yet not less from thence he still must see
   That daily coming, and must hear the goat
Bleating her welcome ; then, towards the sea,
   The happy voices of the playmates float ;

Until, at last, enduring it no more,
He took his wonted station by the door.

Here was, of course, a pitiful surrender ;
   For soon the Child, on whom the Evil Eye
Seemed to exert an influence but slender,
   Would run to question him, till, by and by,
His moody humor like a cloud dispersing,
He found himself uneasily conversing.

That was a sow's-ear, that an egg of skate,
   And this an agate rounded by the wave.
Then came inquiries still more intimate
   About himself, the anvil, and the cave ;
And then, at last, the Child, without alarm
Would even spell the letters on his arm.

" G—A—L—*Galatea.*"   So there grew
   On his part, like some half-remembered tale,
The new-found memory of an ice-bound crew,
   And vague garrulities of spouting whale, —
Of sea-cow basking upon berg and floe.
And Polar light, and stunted Eskimo.

Till, in his heart, which hitherto had been
   Locked as those frozen barriers of the North,
There came once more the season of the green, —
   The tender bud-time and the putting forth,

So that the man, before the new sensation,
Felt for the child a kind of adoration ; —

Rising by night, to search for shell and flower,
    To lay in places where she found them first ;
Hoarding his cherished goat's milk for the hour
    When those young lips might feel the summer's
        thirst ;
Holding himself for all devotion paid
By that clear laughter of the little maid.

Dwelling, alas ! in that fond Paradise
    Where no to-morrow quivers in suspense, —
Where scarce the changes of the sky suffice
    To break the soft forgetfulness of sense, —
Where dreams become realities ; and where
I willingly would leave him — did I dare.

Yet for a little space it still endured,
    Until, upon a day when least of all
The softened Cyclops, by his hopes assured,
    Dreamed the inevitable blow could fall,
Came the stern moment that should all destroy,
Bringing a pert young cockerel of a Boy.

Middy, I think, — he'd "*Acis*" on his box : —
    A black-eyed, sun-burnt, mischief-making imp,

Pet of the mess, — a Puck with curling locks,
    Who straightway travestied the Cyclops' limp,
And marveled how his cousin so could care
For such a "one-eyed, melancholy Bear."

Thus there was war at once; not overt yet,
    For still the Child, unwilling, would not break
The new acquaintanceship, nor quite forget
    The pleasant past; while, for his treasure's
        sake,
The boding smith with clumsy efforts tried
To win the laughing scorner to his side.

There are some sights pathetic; none I know
    More sad than this: to watch a slow-wrought
        mind
Humbling itself, for love, to come and go
    Before some petty tyrant of its kind;
Saddest, ah! — saddest far, — when it can do
Naught to advance the end it has in view.

This was at least the Cyclops' case, until,
    Whether the boy beguiled the Child away,
Or whether that limp Matron on the Hill
    Woke from her novel-reading trance, one day
He waited long and wearily in vain, —
But, from that hour, they never came again.

Yet still he waited, hoping — wondering if
    They still might come, or dreaming that he heard
The sound of far-off voices on the cliff,
    Or starting strangely when the she-goat stirred ;
But nothing broke the silence of the shore,
And, from that hour, the Child returned no more.

Therefore our Cyclops sorrowed, — not as one
    Who can command the gamut of despair ;
But as a man who feels his days are done,
    So dead they seem, — so desolately bare ;
For, though he'd lived a hermit, 'twas but only
Now he discovered that his life was lonely.

The very sea seemed altered, and the shore ;
    The very voices of the air were dumb ;
Time was an emptiness that o'er and o'er
    Ticked with the dull pulsation " Will she
        come ? "
So that he sat " consuming in a dream,"
Much like his old forerunner, Polypheme.

Until there came the question, " Is she gone ? "
    With such sad sick persistence that at last,
Urged by the hungry thought which drove him on,
    Along the steep declivity he passed,

And by the summit panting stood, and still,
Just as the horn was sounding on the hill.

Then, in a dream, beside the " Dragon " door,
  The smith saw travellers standing in the sun ;
Then came the horn again, and three or four
  Looked idly at him from the roof, but One, —
A Child within, — suffused with sudden shame,
Thrust forth a hand, and called to him by name.

Thus the coach vanished from his sight, but he
  Limped back with bitter pleasure in his pain ;
He was not all forgotten — could it be ?
  And yet the knowledge made the memory vain ;
And then — he felt a pressure in his throat,
So, for that night, forgot to milk his goat.

What then might come of silent misery,
  What new resolvings then might intervene,
I know not.   Only, with the morning sky,
  The goat stood tethered on the " Dragon "
    green,
And those who, wondering, questioned thereupon,
Found the hut empty, — for the man was gone.

A STORY FROM A DICTIONARY.

"Sic visum Veneri: cui placet impares
Formas atque animos sub juga aënea
Saevo mittere cum joco."
— HOR. i. 33.

" LOVE mocks us all "—as Horace said of old :
From sheer perversity, that arch-offender
Still yokes unequally the hot and cold,
The short and tall, the hardened and the tender ;
He bids a Socrates espouse a scold,
And makes a Hercules forget his gender : —
Sic visum Veneri ! Lest samples fail,
I add a fresh one from the page of BAYLE.

It was in Athens that the thing occurred,
In the last days of Alexander's rule,
While yet in Grove or Portico was heard
The studious murmur of its learned school ; —
Nay, 'tis one favoured of Minerva's bird
Who plays therein the hero (or the fool)
With a Megarian, who must then have been
A maid, and beautiful, and just eighteen.

I shan't describe her.   Beauty is the same
 In Anno Domini as erst B.C.;
The type is still that witching One who came,
 Between the furrows, from the bitter sea;
'Tis but to shift accessories and frame,
 And this our heroine in a trice would be,
Save that she wore a *peplum* and a *chiton*,
Like any modern on the beach at Brighton.

Stay, I forget !   Of course the sequel shows
 She had some qualities of disposition,
To which, in general, her sex are foes, —
 As strange proclivities to erudition,
And lore unfeminine, reserved for those
 Who now-a-days descant on " Woman's Mis-
  sion,"
Or tread instead that " primrose path " to know-
  ledge,
That milder Academe — the Girton College.

The truth is, she admired . . . . a learned man.
 There were no curates in that sunny Greece,
For whom the mind emotional could plan
 Fine-art habiliments in gold and fleece;
(This was ere chasuble or cope began
 To shake the centres of domestic peace ;)

So that " admiring," such as maids give way to,
Turned to the ranks of Zeno and of Plato.

The "object" here was mildly prepossessing,
    At least, regarded in a woman's sense ;
His *forte*, it seems, lay chiefly in expressing
    Disputed fact in Attic eloquence ;
His ways were primitive ; and as to dressing,
    His toilet was a negative pretence ;
He kept, besides, the *régime* of the Stoic ; —
In short, was not, by any means, " heroic."

Sic visum Veneri ! — The thing is clear.
    Her friends were furious, her lovers nettled ;
'Twas much as though the Lady Vere de Vere
    On some hedge-schoolmaster her heart had
       settled.
Unheard ! Intolerable ! — a lumbering steer
    To plod the upland with a mare high-mettled ! —
They would, no doubt, with far more pleasure
       hand her
To curled Euphorion or Anaximander.

And so they used due discipline, of course,
    To lead to reason this most erring daughter,
Proceeding even to extremes of force, —
    Confinement (solitary), and bread and water ;

Then, having lectured her till they were hoarse,
  Finding that this to no submission brought her,
At last, (unwisely[1]) to the man they sent,
That he might combat her by argument.

Being, they fancied, but a bloodless thing ;
  Or else too well forewarned of that commotion
Which poets feign inseparable from Spring
  To suffer danger from a school-girl notion ;
Also they hoped that she might find her king,
  On close inspection, clumsy and Bœotian : —
This was acute enough, and yet, between us,
I think they thought too little about Venus.

Something, I know, of this sort is related
  In Garrick's life.   However, the man came,
And taking first his mission's end as stated,
  Began at once her sentiments to tame,
Working discreetly to the point debated
  By steps rhetorical I spare to name ;
In other words, — he broke the matter gently.
Meanwhile, the lady looked at him intently,

Wistfully, sadly, — and it put him out,
  Although he went on steadily, but faster.

[1] "Unwisely," surely.   But 'tis well to mention
    That this particular is *not* invention.

There were some maladies he'd read about
    Which seemed, at first, most difficult to master;
They looked intractable at times, no doubt,
    But all they needed was a little plaster;
This was a thing physicians long had pondered,
Considered, weighed . . . . and then . . . . and
      then he wandered.

('Tis so embarrassing to have before you
    A silent auditor, with candid eyes;
With lips that speak no sentence to restore you,
    And aspect, generally, of pained surprise;
Then, if we add that all these things adore you,
    'Tis really difficult to syllogise : —
Of course it mattered not to him a feather,
But still he wished . . . . they'd not been left
      together.)

" Of one," he said, continuing, " of these
    The young especially should be suspicious;
Seeing no ailment in Hippocrates
    Could be at once so tedious and capricious;
No seeming apple of Hesperides
    More fatal, deadlier, and more delicious —
Pernicious, — he should say, — for all its seem-
      ing . ."
It seemed to him he simply was blaspheming.

If she had only turned askance, or uttered
  Word in reply, or trifled with her brooch,
Or sighed, or cried, grown petulant, or fluttered,
    He might (in metaphor) have " called his
      coach ";
Yet still, while patiently he hemmed and stuttered,
  She wore her look of wondering reproach ;
(And those who read the " Shakespeare of Ro-
    mances "
Know of what stuff a girl's "dynamic glance " is.)

" But there was still a cure, the wise insisted,
  In Love, — or rather, in Philosophy.
Philosophy — no, Love — at best existed
  But as an ill for that to remedy :
There was no knot so intricately twisted,
  There was no riddle but at last should be
By Love—he meant Philosophy—resolved . . ."
The truth is, he was getting quite involved.

O sovran Love ! how far thy power surpasses
  Aught that is taught of Logic or the Schools !
Here was a man, " far seen " in all the classes,
  Strengthened of precept, fortified of rules,
Mute as the least articulate of asses ;
  Nay, at an age when every passion cools,

Conscious of nothing but a sudden yearning
Stronger by far than any force of learning!

Therefore he changed his tone, flung down his
    wallet,
  Described his lot, how pitiable and poor;
The hut of mud, — the miserable pallet, —
  The alms solicited from door to door;
The scanty fare of bitter bread and sallet, —
  Could she this shame, — this poverty endure?
I scarcely think he knew what he was doing,
But that last line had quite a touch of wooing.

And so she answered him, — those early Greeks
  Took little care to keep concealment preying
At any length upon their damask cheeks, —
  She answered him by very simply saying,
She could and would : — and said it as one speaks
  Who takes no course without much careful
    weighing. . . .
Was this, perchance, the answer that he hoped?
It might, or might not be. But they eloped.

Sought the free pine-wood and the larger air, —
  The leafy sanctuaries, remote and inner,
Where the great heart of nature, beating bare,
  Receives benignantly both saint and sinner ; —

Leaving propriety to gasp and stare,
   And shake its head, like Burleigh, after dinner,
From pure incompetence to mar or mend them :
They fled and wed ; — though, mind, I don't
   defend them.

I don't defend them.   'Twas a serious act,
   No doubt too much determined by the senses ;
(Alas ! when these affinities attract,
   We lose the future in the present tenses !)
Besides, the least establishment's a fact
   Involving nice adjustment of expenses ;
Moreover, too, reflection should reveal
That not remote contingent — *la famille.*

Yet these, maybe, were happy in their lot.
   Milton has said (and surely Milton knows)
That after all, philosophy is " not, —
   Not harsh and crabbed, as dull fools suppose ; "
And some, no doubt, for Love's sake have forgot
   Much that is needful in this world of prose : —
Perchance 'twas so with these.   But who shall say ?
Time has long since swept them and theirs away.

THE WATER–CURE.

A TALE : IN THE MANNER OF PRIOR.

"—*portentaque Thessala rides ?"*
—HOR.
"— *Thessalian portents do you flout ?"*
*   *

CARDENIO'S fortunes ne'er miscarried
Until the day CARDENIO married.
What then ? the Nymph no doubt was young ?
She was : but yet — she had a tongue !
Most women have, you seem to say.
I grant it — in a different way.

'Twas not that organ half-divine,
With which, Dear Friend, your spouse or mine,
What time we seek our nightly pillows,
Rebukes our easy peccadilloes :
'Twas not so tuneful, so composing ;
'Twas louder and less often dozing ;
At *Ombre, Basset, Loo, Quadrille,*
You heard it resonant and shrill ;
You heard it rising, rising yet
Beyond SELINDA'S parroquet ;

178

You heard it rival and outdo
The chair-men and the link-boy too ;
In short, wherever lungs perform,
Like MARLBOROUGH, it rode the storm.

So uncontrolled it came to be,
CARDENIO feared his *chère amie*
(Like ECHO by *Cephissus* shore)
Would turn to voice and nothing more.

That ('tis conceded) must be cured
Which can't by practice be endured.
CARDENIO, though he loved the maid,
Grew daily more and more afraid ;
And since advice could not prevail
(Reproof but seemed to fan the gale),
A prudent man, he cast about
To find some fitting nostrum out.
What need to say that priceless drug
Had not in any mine been dug ?
What need to say no skilful leech
Could check that plethora of speech ?
Suffice it, that one lucky day
CARDENIO tried — another way.

A Hermit (there were hermits then ;
The most accessible of men !)

Near *Vauxhall's* sacred shade resided;
In him, at length, our friend confided.
(Simples, for show, he used to sell ;
But cast *Nativities* as well.)
Consulted, he looked wondrous wise ;
Then undertook the enterprise.

What that might be, the Muse must spare :
To tell the truth, she was not there.
She scorns to patch what she ignores
With *Similes* and *Metaphors ;*
And so, in short, to change the scene,
She slips a fortnight in between.

Behold our pair then (quite by chance !)
In *Vauxhall's* garden of romance, —
That paradise of nymphs and grottoes,
Of fans, and fiddles, and ridottoes !
What wonder if, the lamps reviewed,
The song encored, the maze pursued,
No further feat could seem more pat
Than seek the Hermit after that ?
Who then more keen her fate to see
Than this, the new Leuconoë,
On fire to learn the lore forbidden
In Babylonian numbers hidden ?

Forthwith they took the darkling road
To ALBUMAZAR his abode.

Arriving, they beheld the sage
Intent on hieroglyphic page,
In high *Armenian* cap arrayed
And girt with engines of his trade ;
(As *Skeletons*, and *Spheres*, and *Cubes ;*
As *Amulets* and *Optic Tubes ;*)
With dusky depths behind revealing
Strange shapes that dangled from the ceiling ;
While more to palsy the beholder
A Black Cat sat upon his shoulder.

The Hermit eyed the Lady o'er
As one whose face he'd seen before ;
And then, with agitated looks,
He fell to fumbling at his books.

CARDENIO felt his spouse was frightened,
Her grasp upon his arm had tightened ;
Judge then her horror and her dread
When " Vox Stellarum " shook his head ;
Then darkly spake in phrase forlorn
Of *Taurus* and of *Capricorn ;*
Of stars averse, and stars ascendant,
And stars entirely independent ;

In fact, it seemed that all the Heavens
Were set at sixes and at sevens,
Portending, in her case, some fate
Too fearful to prognosticate.

    Meanwhile the Dame was well-nigh dead.
" But is there naught," CARDENIO said,
" No sign or token, Sage, to show
From whence, or what, this dismal woe ? "

    The Sage, with circle and with plane,
Betook him to his charts again.
" It vaguely seems to threaten Speech :
No more (he said) the signs can teach."

    But still CARDENIO tried once more :
" Is there no potion in your store,
No charm by *Chaldee* mage concerted
By which this doom can be averted ? "

    The Sage, with motion doubly mystic,
Resumed his juggling cabalistic.
The aspects here again were various ;
But seemed to indicate *Aquarius.*
Thereat portentously he frowned ;
Then frowned again, then smiled ;—'twas found!

But 'twas too simple to be tried.
" What is it, then ? " at once they cried.

" Whene'er by chance you feel incited
To speak at length, or uninvited ;
Whene'er you feel your tones grow shrill
(At times, we know, the softest will l),
This word oracular, my daughter,
Bids you to fill your mouth with water :
Further, to hold it firm and fast,
Until the danger be o'erpast."

The Dame, by this in part relieved
The prospect of escape perceived,
Rebelled a little at the diet.
CARDENIO said discreetly, " Try it,
Try it, my Own. You have no choice,
What if you lose your charming voice l "
She tried, it seems. And whether then
Some god stepped in, benign to men ;
Or Modesty, too long outlawed,
Contrived to aid the pious fraud,-
I know not : — but from that same day
She talked in quite a different way.

THE NOBLE PATRON.

" Ce sont les amours
Que font les beaux jours."

WHAT is a *Patron?* JOHNSON knew,
   And well that lifelike portrait drew.
He is a Patron who looks down
With careless eye on men who drown;
But if they chance to reach the land,
Encumbers them with helping hand.
Ah! happy we whose artless rhyme
No longer now must creep to climb!
Ah! happy we of later days,
Who 'scape those *Caudine Forks* of praise!
Whose votive page may dare commend
A Brother, or a private Friend!
Not so it fared with scribbling man,
As POPE says, " under my Queen ANNE."

DICK DOVECOT (this was long, be sure,
Ere he attained his *Wiltshire* cure,
And settled down, like humbler folks,
To cowslip wine and country jokes)
Once hoped — as who will not? — for fame,
And dreamed of honours and a Name.

184

A fresh-cheek'd lad, he came to Town
In homespun hose and russet brown,
But armed at point with every view
Enforced in RAPIN and BOSSU,
Besides a stout portfolio ripe
For LINTOT's or for TONSON's type.
He went the rounds, saw all the sights,
Dropped in at *Will's* and *Tom's* o' nights ;
Heard BURNET preach, saw BICKNELL dance,
E'en gained from ADDISON a glance ;
Nay, once, to make his bliss complete,
He supp'd with STEELE in *Bury Street.*
('Tis true the feast was half by stealth :
PRUE was in bed : they drank her health.)

By this his purse was running low,
And he must either print or go.
He went to TONSON.   TONSON said —
Well !   TONSON hummed and shook his head ;
Deplor'd the times ; abus'd the Town ;
But thought — at length — it might go down ;
With aid, of course, of *Elzevir*,
And *Prologue* to a Prince, or Peer.
Dick winced at this, for adulation
Was scarce that candid youth's vocation :
Nor did he deem his rustic lays
Required a *Coronet* for *Bays.*

But there — the choice was that, or none.
The Lord was found ; the thing was done.
With HORACE and with TOOKE's *Pantheon*,
He penn'd his tributary pæan ;
Despatched his gift, nor waited long
The meed of his ingenuous song.

Ere two days pass'd, a hackney chair
Brought a pert spark with languid air,
A lace cravat about his throat, —
Brocaded gown, — *en papillotes*.
("My Lord himself," quoth DICK, "at least ! "
But no, 'twas that " inferior priest,"
His Lordship's man.)   He held a card :
My Lord (it said) would see the Bard.

The day arrived ; DICK went, was shown
Into an anteroom, alone —
A great gilt room with mirrored door,
Festoons of flowers and marble floor,
Whose lavish splendours made him look
More shabby than a sheepskin book.
(His own book — by the way — he spied
On a far table, toss'd aside.)

DICK waited, as they only wait
Who haunt the chambers of the Great.

He heard the chairmen come and go ;
He heard the Porter yawn below ;
Beyond him, in the Grand Saloon,
He heard the silver stroke of noon,
And thought how at this very time
The old church clock at home would chime.
Dear heart, how plain he saw it all !
The lich-gate and the crumbling wall,
The stream, the pathway to the wood,
The bridge where they so oft had stood.
Then, in a trice, both church and clock
Vanish'd before . . . a shuttlecock.

A shuttlecock !   And following slow
The zigzag of its to-and-fro,
And so intent upon its flight
She neither look'd to left nor right,
Came a tall girl with floating hair,
Light as a wood-nymph, and as fair.

O Dea certé ! — thought poor Dick,
And thereupon his memories quick
Ran back to her who flung the ball
In Homer's page, and next to all
The dancing maids that bards have sung ;
Lastly to One at home, as young,

As fresh, as light of foot, and glad,
Who, when he went, had seem'd so sad.
O Dea certé ! (Still, he stirred
Nor hand nor foot, nor uttered word.)

Meanwhile the shuttlecock in air
Went darting gaily here and there ;
Now crossed a mirror's face, and next
Shot up amidst the sprawl'd, perplex'd
Olympus overhead.   At last,
Jerk'd sidelong by a random cast,
The striker miss'd it, and it fell
Full on the book DICK knew so well.

(If he had thought to speak or bow,
Judge if he moved a muscle now !)

The player paused, bent down to look,
Lifted a cover of the book ;
Pished at the Prologue, passed it o'er,
Went forward for a page or more
(*Asem and Asa :* DICK could trace
Almost the passage and the place) ;
Then for a moment with bent head
Rested upon her hand and read.

(DICK thought once more how cousin CIS
Used when she read to lean like this ; —
" Used when she *read*," — why, CIS could *say*
All he had written, — any day !)

Sudden was heard a hurrying tread ;
The great doors creaked.   The reader fled.
Forth came a crowd with muffled laughter,
A waft of Bergamot, and after,
His Chaplain smirking at his side,
My Lord himself in all his pride —
A portly shape in stars and lace,
With wine-bag cheeks and vacant face.

DICK bowed and smiled.   The Great Man
        stared,
With look half puzzled and half scared ;
Then seemed to recollect, turned round,
And mumbled some imperfect sound :
A moment more, his coach of state
Dipped on its springs beneath his weight ;
And DICK, who followed at his heels,   ·
Heard but the din of rolling wheels.

Away, too, all his dreams had rolled ;
And yet they left him half consoled :

Fame, after all, he thought might wait.
Would CIS? Suppose he were too late!
Ten months he'd lost in Town — an age!

Next day he took the *Wiltshire* Stage.

VERS DE SOCIETÉ.

191

INCOGNITA.

JUST for a space that I met her —
    Just for a day in the train !
It began when she feared it would wet her,
    That tiniest spurtle of rain :
So we tucked a great rug in the sashes,
    And carefully padded the pane ;
And I sorrow in sackcloth and ashes,
    Longing to do it again !

Then it grew when she begged me to reach her
    A dressing-case under the seat ;
She was " really so tiny a creature,
    That she needed a stool for her feet ! "
Which was promptly arranged to her order
    With a care that was even minute,
And a glimpse — of an open-work border,
    And a glance — of the fairyest boot.

Then it drooped, and revived at some hovels —
    " Were they houses for men or for pigs ? "
Then it shifted to muscular novels,
    With a little digression on prigs :

She thought " Wives and Daughters " " *so* jolly ; "
  " Had I read it ? " She knew when I had,
Like the rest, I should dote upon " Molly ; "
  And " poor Mrs. Gaskell — how sad ! "

" Like Browning ? " " But so-so." His proof lay
  Too deep for her frivolous mood,
That preferred your mere metrical *soufflé*
  To the stronger poetical food ;
Yet at times he was good — " as a tonic : "
  Was Tennyson writing just now ?
And was this new poet Byronic,
  And clever, and naughty, or how ?

Then we trifled with concerts and croquêt,
  Then she daintily dusted her face ;
Then she sprinkled herself with " Ess Bouquet,"
  Fished out from the foregoing case ;
And we chattered of Gassier and Grisi,
  And voted Aunt Sally a bore ;
Discussed if the tight rope were easy,
  Or Chopin much harder than Spohr.

And oh ! the odd things that she quoted,
  With the prettiest possible look,
And the price of two buns that she noted
  In the prettiest possible book ;

While her talk like a musical rillet
   Flashed on with the hours that flew,
And the carriage, her smile seemed to fill it
   With just enough summer — for Two.

Till at last in her corner, peeping
   From a nest of rugs and of furs,
With the white shut eyelids sleeping
   On those dangerous looks of hers,
She seemed like a snow-drop breaking,
   Not wholly alive nor dead,
But with one blind impulse making
   To the sounds of the spring overhead ;

And I watched in the lamplight's swerving
   The shade of the down-dropt lid,
And the lip-line's delicate curving,
   Where a slumbering smile lay hid,
Till I longed that, rather than sever,
   The train should shriek into space,
And carry us onward — for ever, —
   Me and that beautiful face.

But she suddenly woke in a fidget,
   With fears she was " nearly at home,"
And talk of a certain Aunt Bridget,
   Whom I mentally wished — well, at Rome ;

Got out at the very next station,
 Looking back with a merry *Bon Soir,*
Adding, too, to my utter vexation,
 A surplus, unkind *Au Revoir.*

So left me to muse on her graces,
 To dose and to muse, till I dreamed
That we sailed through the sunniest places
 In a glorified galley, it seemed ;
But the cabin was made of a carriage,
 And the ocean was Eau-de-Cologne,
And we split on a rock labelled MARRIAGE,
 And I woke, — as cold as a stone.

And that's how I lost her — a jewel,
 Incognita — one in a crowd,
Nor prudent enough to be cruel,
 Nor worldly enough to be proud.
It was just a shut lid and its lashes,
 Just a few hours in a train,
And I sorrow in sackcloth and ashes
 Longing to see her again.

DORA *VERSUS* ROSE.

" The Case is proceeding."

FROM the tragic-est novels at Mudie's —
  At least, on a practical plan —
To the tales of mere Hodges and Judys,
  One love is enough for a man.
But no case that I ever yet met is
  Like mine : I am equally fond
Of Rose, who a charming brunette is,
  And Dora, a blonde.

Each rivals the other in powers —
  Each waltzes, each warbles, each paints —
Miss Rose, chiefly tumble-down towers ;
  Miss Do., perpendicular saints.
In short, to distinguish is folly ;
  'Twixt the pair I am come to the pass
Of Macheath, between Lucy and Polly, —
  Or Buridan's ass.

If it happens that Rosa I've singled
  For a soft celebration in rhyme,

Then the ringlets of Dora get mingled
    Somehow with the tune and the time ;
Or I painfully pen me a sonnet
    To an eyebrow intended for Do.'s,
And behold I am writing upon it
                The legend " To Rose."

Or I try to draw Dora (my blotter
    Is all overscrawled with her head),
If I fancy at last that I've got her,
    It turns to her rival instead ;
Or I find myself placidly adding
    To the rapturous tresses of Rose
Miss Dora's bud-mouth, and her madding,
                Ineffable nose.

Was there ever so sad a dilemma ?
    For Rose I would perish (*pro tem.*) ;
For Dora I'd willingly stem a —
    (Whatever might offer to stem) ;
But to make the invidious election, —
    To declare that on either one's side
I've a scruple, — a grain, more affection,
                I *cannot* decide.

And, as either so hopelessly nice is,
    My sole and my final resource

Is to wait some indefinite crisis, —
  Some feat of molecular force,
To solve me this riddle conducive
  By no means to peace or repose,
Since the issue can scarce be inclusive
              Of Dora *and* Rose.

(Afterthought.)

But, perhaps, if a third (say a Norah),
  Not quite so delightful as Rose, —
Not wholly so charming as Dora, —
  Should appear, is it wrong to suppose, —
As the claims of the others are equal, —
  And flight — in the main — is the best, —
That I might . . . But no matter, — the sequel
            Is easily guessed.

AD ROSAM.

" Mitte sectari ROSA *quo locorum*
Sera moretur."
—HOR. I. 38.

I HAD a vacant dwelling —
　Where situated, I,
As naught can serve the telling,
　Decline to specify ; —
Enough 'twas neither haunted,
　Entailed, nor out of date ;
I put up " Tenant Wanted,"
　And left the rest to Fate.

Then, Rose, you passed the window, —
　I see you passing yet, —
Ah, what could I within do,
　When, Rose, our glances met !
You snared me, Rose, with ribbons,
　Your rose-mouth made me thrall,
Brief — briefer far than Gibbon's,
　Was my " Decline and Fall."

AD ROSAM.

I heard the summons spoken
   That all hear — king and clown :
You smiled — the ice'was broken ;
   You stopped — the bill was down.
How blind we are !   It never
   Occurred to me to seek
If you had come for ever,
   Or only for a week.

The words your voice neglected,
   Seemed written in your eyes ;
The thought your heart protected,
   Your cheek told, missal-wise ; —
I read the rubric plainly
   As any Expert could ;
In short, we dreamed, — insanely,
   As only lovers should.

I broke the tall Œnone,
   That then my chambers graced,
Because she seemed " too bony,"
   To suit your purist taste ;
And you, without vexation,
   May certainly confess
Some graceful approbation,
   Designed à mon adresse.

VERS DE SOCIÉTÉ.

You liked me then, *carina*, —
    You liked me then, I think ;
For your sake gall had been a
    Mere tonic-cup to drink ;
For your sake, bonds were trivial,
    The rack, a *tour-de-force ;*
And banishment, convivial, —
    You coming too, of course.

Then, Rose, a word in jest meant
    Would throw you in a state
That no well-timed investment
    Could quite alleviate ;
Beyond a Paris trousseau
    You prized my smile, I know,
I, yours — ah, more than Rousseau
    The lip of d'Houdetot.

Then, Rose, — But why pursue it ?
    When Fate begins to frown
Best write the final " *fuit,*"
    And gulp the physic down.
And yet, — and yet, that only,
    The song should end with this : —
You left me, — left me lonely,
    Rosa mutabilis !

Left me, with Time for Mentor,
    (A dreary *tête-à-tête !*)
To pen my " Last Lament," or
    Extemporize to Fate,
In blankest verse disclosing
    My bitterness of mind, —
Which is, I learn, composing
    In cases of the kind.

No, Rose.   Though you refuse me,
    Culture the pang prevents ;
" I am not made "— excuse me —
    " Of so slight elements ; "
I leave to common lovers
    The hemlock or the hood ;
My rarer soul recovers
    In dreams of public good.

The Roses of this nation —
    Or so I understand
From careful computation —
    Exceed the gross demand ;
And, therefore, in civility
    To maids that can't be matched,
No man of sensibility
    Should linger unattached.

So, without further fashion —
    A modern Curtius,
Plunging, from pure compassion,
    To aid the overplus, —
I sit down, sad — not daunted,
    And, in my weeds, begin
A new card — " Tenant Wanted ;
    Particulars within."

OUTWARD BOUND.

(HORACE, III. 7.)

" Quid fles, Asterie, quem tibi candidi
Primo restituent vere Favonii —
Gygen ? "

COME, Laura, patience. Time and Spring
　　Your absent Arthur back shall bring,
Enriched with many an Indian thing
　　　　Once more to woo you ;
Him neither wind nor wave can check,
Who, cramped beneath the " Simla's " deck,
Still constant, though with stiffened neck,
　　　　Makes verses to you.

Would it were wave and wind alone !
The terrors of the torrid zone,
The indiscriminate cyclone,
　　　　A man might parry ;
But only faith, or " triple brass,"
Can help the " outward-bound " to pass
Safe through that eastward-faring class
　　　　Who sail to marry.

For him fond mothers, stout and fair,
Ascend the tortuous cabin stair
Only to hold around his chair
  Insidious sessions ;
For him the eyes of daughters droop
Across the plate of handed soup,
Suggesting seats upon the poop,
  And soft confessions.

Nor are these all his pains, nor most.
Romancing captains cease to boast —
Loud majors leave their whist — to roast
  The youthful griffin ;
All, all with pleased persistence show
His fate, — " remote, unfriended, slow," —
His " melancholy " bungalow, —
  His lonely tiffin.

In vain. Let doubts assail the weak ;
Unmoved and calm as "Adam's Peak,"
Your "blameless Arthur" hears them speak
  Of woes that wait him ;
Naught can subdue his soul secure ;
"Arthur will come again," be sure,
Though matron shrewd and maid mature
  Conspire to mate him.

But, Laura, on your side, forbear
To greet with too impressed an air
A certain youth with chestnut hair, —
    A youth unstable;
Albeit none more skilled can guide
The frail canoe on Thamis tide,
Or, trimmer-footed, lighter glide
    Through "Guards" or "Mabel."

Be warned in time. Without a trace
Of acquiescence on your face,
Hear, in the waltz's breathing-space,
    His airy patter;
Avoid the confidential nook;
If, when you sing, you find his look
Grow tender, close your music-book,
    And end the matter.

IN THE ROYAL ACADEMY.

HUGH (on *furlough*).   HELEN (*his cousin*).

HELEN.

THEY have not come ! And ten is past,—
   Unless, by chance, my watch is fast ;
—Aunt Mabel surely told us " ten."

HUGH.

I doubt if she can do it, then.
In fact, their train . . . .

HELEN.

         That is, — you knew.
How could you be so treacherous, Hugh ?

HUGH.

Nay ; — it is scarcely mine, the crime,
One can't account for railway-time !
Where shall we sit ? Not here, I vote ; —
At least, there's nothing here of note.

HELEN.

Then *here* we'll stay, please.   Once for all,
I bar all artists, — great and small !
From now until we go in June
I shall hear nothing but this tune : —
Whether I like Long's " Vashti," or
Like Leslie's " Naughty Kitty " more ;
With all that critics, right or wrong,
Have said of Leslie and of Long . . . .
No.   If you value my esteem,
I beg you'll take another theme ;
Paint me some pictures, if you will,
But spare me these, for good and ill . . . .

HUGH.

" Paint you some pictures ! "   Come, that's kind !
You know I'm nearly colour-blind.

HELEN.

Paint then, in words.   You did before ;
Scenes at — where was it ?   Dustypoor ?
You know . . . .

HUGH (*with an inspiration*).
I'll try.

HELEN.

But mind they're pretty
Not " hog hunts." . . . .

HUGH.

You shall be Committee,
And say if they are " out " or " in."

HELEN.

I shall reject them all.   Begin.

HUGH.

Here is the first.   An antique Hall
(Like Chanticlere) with panelled wall.
A boy, or rather lad.   A girl,
Laughing with all her rows of pearl
Before a portrait in a ruff.
He meanwhile watches . . . .

HELEN.

That's enough,
It wants " *verve*," " *brio*," " breadth," " de-
sign," . . . .
Besides, it's English.   I decline.

HUGH.

This is the next.   'Tis finer far:
A foaming torrent (say Braemar).

A pony, grazing by a boulder,
Then the same pair, a little older,
Left by some lucky chance together.
He begs her for a sprig of heather . . . .

HELEN.
— " Which she accords with smile seraphic."
I know it, — it was in the "Graphic."
Declined.

HUGH.
Once more, and I forego
All hopes of hanging, high or low :
Behold the hero of the scene,
In bungalow and palankeen . . . .

HELEN.
What ! — all at once ! But that's absurd ; —
Unless he's Sir Boyle Roche's bird !

HUGH.
Permit me — 'Tis a Panorama,
In which the person of the drama,
Mid orientals dusk and tawny,
Mid warriors drinking brandy pawnee,
Mid scorpions, dowagers, and griffins,

In morning rides, at noon-day tiffins,
In every kind of place and weather,
Is solaced . . . . by a sprig of heather.
          (More seriously.)
He puts that faded scrap before
The " Rajah," or the " Koh-i-noor " . . . .
He would not barter it for all
Benares, or the Taj-Mahal . .
It guides, —directs his every act,
And word, and thought — In short — in fact —
I mean . . . .
          (Opening his locket.)
      Look, Helen, that's the heather !
(Too late ! Here come both Aunts together.)

HELEN.

What heather, Sir ?
        (After a pause.)
          And why . . . . " too late ? "
— Aunt Dora, how you've made us wait !
Don't you agree that it's a pity
Portraits are hung by the Committee ?

THE LAST DESPATCH.

HURRAH ! the Season's past at last ;
    At length we've " done " our pleasure.
Dear " Pater," if you *only* knew
How much I've *longed* for home and you, —
    Our own green lawn and leisure !

And then the pets ! One half forgets
    The dear dumb friends — in Babel.
I hope my special fish is fed ; —
I long to see poor Nigra's head
    Pushed at me from the stable !

I long to see the cob and " Rob," —
    Old Bevis and the Collie ;
And *won't* we read in " Traveller's Rest " !
Home readings after all are best ; —
    None else seem half so " jolly ! "

One misses your dear kindly store
    Of fancies quaint and funny ;
One misses, too, your kind *bon-mot ;* —
The Mayfair wit I mostly know
    Has more of gall than honey !

How tired one grows of " calls and balls ! "
    This " *toujours perdrix* " wearies ;
I'm longing, quite, for " Notes on Knox ";
(*Apropos*, I've the loveliest box
    For holding *Notes and Queries !*)

A change of place would suit my case.
    You'll take me ? — on probation ?
As " Lady-help," then, let it be ;
I feel (as Lavender shall see),
    That Jams are *my* vocation !

How's Lavender ? My love to her.
    Does Briggs still flirt with Flowers ? —
Has Hawthorn stubbed the common clear ? —
You'll let me give *some* picnics, Dear,
    And ask the Vanes and Towers ?

I met Belle Vane. " HE's " still in Spain !
    Sir John won't let them marry.
Aunt drove the boys to Brompton Rink ;
And Charley, — changing Charley, — think,
    Is now *au mieux* with Carry !

And NO. You know what " *No* " I mean —
    There's no one yet at present :
The Benedick I have in view

Must be a something wholly new, —
One's father's *far* too pleasant.

So hey, I say, for home and you !
Good-by to Piccadilly ;
Balls, beaux, and Bolton-row, adieu !
Expect me, Dear, at half-past two ;
Till then, — your Own Fond — Milly.

" PREMIERS AMOURS."

Old Loves and old dreams, —
" Requiescant in pace."
How strange now it seems, —
" Old " Loves and " old " dreams !
Yet we once wrote you reams
Maude, Alice, and Gracie !
Old Loves and old dreams, —
" Requiescant in pace."

WHEN I called at the " Hollies " to-day,
    In the room with the cedar-wood presses,
Aunt Deb. was just folding away
    What she calls her " memorial dresses."

She'd the frock that she wore at fifteen, —
    Short-waisted, of course — my abhorrence ;
She'd " the loveliest " — something in " een "
    That she wears in her portrait by Lawrence ;

She'd the " jelick " she used — "as a Greek," (!)
    She'd the habit she got her bad fall in ;
She had e'en the blue *moiré antique*
    That she opened Squire Grasshopper's ball
        in : —

New and old they were all of them there : —
   Sleek velvet and bombazine stately, —
She had hung them each over a chair
   To the " *paniers* " she's taken to lately

(Which she showed me, I think, by mistake).
   And I conned o'er the forms and the fashions,
Till the faded old shapes seemed to wake
   All the ghosts of my passed-away "pas-
      sions ; " —

From the days of love's youthfullest dream,
   When the height of my shooting idea
Was to burn, like a young Polypheme,
   For a somewhat mature Galatea.

There was Lucy, who " tiffed " with her first,
   And who threw me as soon as her third came ;
There was Norah, whose cut was the worst,
   For she told me to wait till my " berd " came ;

Pale Blanche, who subsisted on salts ;
   Blonde Bertha, who doted on Schiller ;
Poor Amy, who taught me to waltz ;
   Plain Ann, that I wooed for the " siller ; " —

All danced round my head in a ring,
   Like " The Zephyrs " that somebody painted,

All shapes of the feminine thing —
   Shy, scornful, seductive, and sainted, —

To my Wife, in the days she was young . . .
   " How, Sir," says that lady, disgusted,
" Do you dare to include ME among
   Your loves that have faded and rusted ? "

" Not at all ! " — I benignly retort.
   (I was just the least bit in a temper !)
" Those, alas ! were the fugitive sort,
   But you are my — *eadem semper !* "

Full stop, — and a Sermon.   Yet think, —
   There was surely good ground for a quarrel, —
She had checked me when just on the brink
   Of — I feel — a remarkable MORAL.

THE SCREEN IN THE LUMBER ROOM.

Y ES, here it is, behind the box,
    That puzzle wrought so neatly —
That paradise of paradox —
    We once knew so completely;
You see it ? 'Tis the same, I swear,
    Which stood, that chill September,
Beside your aunt Lavinia's chair
    The year when . . . You remember?

Look, Laura, look ! You must recall
    This florid " Fairy's Bower,"
This wonderful Swiss waterfall,
    And this old " Leaning Tower ; "
And here's the " Maiden of Cashmere,"
    And here is Bewick's " Starling,"
And here the dandy cuirassier
    You thought was " such a Darling ! "

Your poor dear Aunt ! you know her way,
    She used to say this figure
Reminded her of Count D'Orsay
    " In all his youthful vigour ; "

219

And here's the " cot beside the hill "
  We chose for habitation,
The day that . . . But I doubt if still
  You'd like the situation !

Too damp — by far !　She little knew,
  Your guileless Aunt Lavinia,
Those evenings when she slumbered through
  " The Prince of Abyssinia,"
That there were two beside her chair
  Who both had quite decided
To see things in a rosier air
  Than Rasselas provided !

Ah ! men wore stocks in Britain's land,
  And maids short waists and tippets,
When this old-fashioned screen was planned
  From hoarded scraps and snippets ;
But more — far more, I think — to me
  Than those who first designed it,
Is this — in Eighteen Seventy-Three
  I kissed you first behind it.

DAISY'S VALENTINES.

A LL night through Daisy's sleep, it seems,
　　Have ceaseless "rat-tats" thundered;
All night through Daisy's rosy dreams
　　Have devious Postmen blundered,
Delivering letters round her bed, —
Mysterious missives, sealed with red,
And franked of course with due Queen's-head, —
　　While Daisy lay and wondered.

But now, when chirping birds begin,
　　And Day puts off the Quaker, —
When Cook renews her morning din,
　　And rates the cheerful baker, —
She dreams her dream no dream at all;
For, just as pigeons come at call,
Winged letters flutter down, and fall
　　Around her head, and wake her.

Yes, there they are ! With quirk and twist,
　　And fraudful arts directed;
(Save Grandpapa's dear stiff old " fist,"
　　Through all disguise detected ;)

221

But which is his, — her young Lothair's, —
Who wooed her on the school-room stairs
With three sweet cakes, and two ripe pears,
 In one neat pile collected?

'Tis there, be sure. Though truth to speak,
 (If truth may be permitted),
I doubt that young " gift-bearing Greek "
 Is scarce for fealty fitted;
For has he not (I grieve to say),
To two loves more, on this same day,
In just this same emblazoned way,
 His transient vows transmitted?

He *may* be true. Yet, Daisy dear,
 That even youth grows colder
You'll find is no new thing, I fear;
 And when you're somewhat older,
You'll read of one Dardanian boy
Who " wooed with gifts " a maiden coy, —
Then took the morning train to Troy,
 In spite of all he'd told her.

But wait. Your time will come. And then,
 Obliging Fates, please send her
The bravest thing you have in men,
 Sound-hearted, strong, and tender; —

The kind of man, dear Fates, you know,
That feels how shyly Daisies grow,
And what soft things they are, and so
   Will spare to spoil or mend her.

IN TOWN.

" The blue fly sung in the pane." — TENNYSON.

TOILING in Town now is " horrid,"
   (There is that woman again !) —
June in the zenith is torrid,
   Thought gets dry in the brain.

There is that woman again :
   " Strawberries ! fourpence a pottle ! "
Thought gets dry in the brain ;
   Ink gets dry in the bottle.

" Strawberries ! fourpence a pottle ! "
   Oh for the green of a lane ! —
Ink gets dry in the bottle ;
   " Buzz " goes a fly in the pane !

Oh for the green of a lane,
   Where one might lie and be lazy !
" Buzz " goes a fly in the pane ;
   Bluebottles drive me crazy !

Where one might lie and be lazy,
    Careless of Town and all in it ! —
Bluebottles drive me crazy :
    I shall go mad in a minute !

Careless of Town and all in it,
    With some one to soothe and to still you ; —
I shall go mad in a minute ;
    Bluebottle, then I shall kill you !

With some one to soothe and to still you,
    As only one's feminine kin do, —
Bluebottle, then I shall kill you :
    There now ! I've broken the window !

As only one's feminine kin do, —
    Some muslin-clad Mabel or May ! —
There now ! I've broken the window !
    Bluebottle's off and away !

Some muslin-clad Mabel or May,
    To dash one with eau de Cologne ; —
Bluebottle's off and away ;
    And why should I stay here alone !

To dash one with eau de Cologne,
   All over one's eminent forehead ; —
And why should I stay here alone !
   Toiling in Town now is " horrid."

A SONNET IN DIALOGUE.

FRANK (*on the Lawn*).
COME to the Terrace, May, — the sun is low.

MAY (*in the House*).
Thanks, I prefer my Browning here instead.

FRANK.
There are two peaches by the strawberry bed.

MAY.
They will be riper if we let them grow.

FRANK.
Then the Park-aloe is in bloom, you know.

MAY.
Also, her Majesty Queen Anne is dead.

FRANK.
But surely, May, your pony must be fed.

227

MAY.

And was, and is.   I fed him hours ago.
'Tis useless, Frank, you see I shall not stir.

FRANK.

Still, I had something you would like to hear.

MAY.

No doubt some new frivolity of men.

FRANK.

Nay, — 'tis a thing the gentler sex deplores
Chiefly, I think . . .

MAY (*coming to the window*).
What is this secret, then?

FRANK (*mysteriously*).
There are no eyes more beautiful than yours!

GROWING GRAY.

"On a l'âge de son cœur." — A. D'HOUDETOT.

A LITTLE more toward the light ; —
    Me miserable !   Here's one that's white ;
        And one that's turning ;
Adieu to song and " salad days ; "
My Muse, let's go at once to Jay's,
        And order mourning.

We must reform our rhymes, my Dear, —
Renounce the gay for the severe, —
        Be grave, not witty ;
We have, no more, the right to find
That Pyrrha's hair is neatly twined, —
        That Chloe's pretty.

Young Love's for us a farce that's played ;
Light canzonet and serenade
        No more may tempt us ;
Gray hairs but ill accord with dreams ;
From aught but sour didactic themes
        Our years exempt us.

Indeed ! you really fancy so ?
You think for one white streak we grow
      At once satiric ?
A fiddlestick ! Each hair's a string
To which our ancient Muse shall sing
      A younger lyric.

The heart's still sound. Shall " cakes and ale "
Grow rare to youth because *we* rail
      At schoolboy dishes ?
Perish the thought ! 'Tis ours to chant
When neither Time nor Tide can grant
      Belief with wishes.

VARIA.

THE MALTWORM'S MADRIGAL.

I DRINK of the Ale of Southwark, I drink of
the Ale of Chepe ;
At noon I dream on the settle ; at night I cannot
sleep ;
For my love, my love it groweth ; I waste me all
the day ;
And when I see sweet Alison, I know not what
to say.

The sparrow when he spieth his Dear upon the
tree,
He beateth-to his little wing ; he chirketh lustily ;
But when I see sweet Alison, the words begin to
fail ;
I wot that I shall die of Love — an I die not of
Ale.

Her lips are like the muscadel ; her brows are
black as ink ;
Her eyes are bright as beryl stones that in the
tankard wink ;

But when she sees me coming, she shrilleth out
    —"Te-Hee!
Fye on thy ruddy nose, Cousin, what lackest thou
    of me?"

"Fye on thy ruddy nose, Cousin! Why be thine
    eyes so small?
Why go thy legs tap-lappetty like men that fear to
    fall?
Why is thy leathern doublet besmeared with stain
    and spot?
Go to. Thou art no man (she saith) — thou art
    a Pottle-pot!"

"No man," i'faith. "No man!" she saith.
    And "Pottle-pot" thereto!
"Thou sleepest like our dog all day; thou
    drink'st as fishes do."
I would that I were Tibb the dog; he wags at
    her his tail;
Or would that I were fish, perdy, and all the sea
    were Ale!

So I drink of the Ale of Southwark, I drink of
    the Ale of Chepe;

All day I dream in the sunlight ; I dream and eke
    I weep,
But little lore of loving can any flagon teach,
For when my tongue is looséd most, then most I
    lose my speech.

AN APRIL PASTORAL.

He.

WHITHER away, fair Neat-herdess?
  She. Shepherd, I go to tend my kine.
He. Stay thou, and watch this flock of mine.
She. With thee? Nay, that were idleness.
He. Thy kine will pasture none the less.
She. Not so: they wait me and my sign.
He. I'll pipe to thee beneath the pine.
She. Thy pipe will soothe not their distress.
He. Dost thou not hear beside the spring
  How the gay birds are carolling?
She. I hear them. But it may not be.
He. Farewell then, Sweetheart! Farewell now.
She. Shepherd, farewell —— Where goest thou?
He. I go .. to tend thy kine for thee!

A NEW SONG OF THE SPRING GARDENS.

To the Burden of "Rogues All."

COME hither ye gallants, come hither ye maids,
　　To the trim gravelled walks, to the shady
　　　　arcades;
Come hither, come hither, the nightingales call; —
Sing *Tantarara,* — Vauxhall! Vauxhall!

Come hither, ye cits, from your Lothbury hives!
Come hither, ye husbands, and look to your
　　wives!
For the sparks are as thick as the leaves in the
　　Mall; —
Sing *Tantarara,* — Vauxhall! Vauxhall!

Here the 'prentice from Aldgate may ogle a
　　Toast!
Here his Worship must elbow the knight of the
　　post!
For the wicket is free to the great and the small; —
Sing *Tantarara,* — Vauxhall! Vauxhall!

Here Betty may flaunt in her mistress's sack !
Here Trip wear his master's brocade on his back !
Here a hussy may ride, and a rogue take the
      wall ; —
Sing *Tantarara,* — Vauxhall ! Vauxhall !

Here Beauty may grant, and here Valour may ask !
Here the plainest may pass for a Belle (in a
      mask) !
Here a domino covers the short and the tall ; —
Sing *Tantarara,* — Vauxhall ! Vauxhall !

'Tis a type of the world, with its drums and its din ;
'Tis a type of the world, for when once you come in
You are loth to go out ; like the world 'tis a ball ; —
Sing *Tantarara,* — Vauxhall ! Vauxhall !

A LOVE-SONG.

(XVIII. CENT.)

WHEN first in CELIA's ear I poured
  A yet unpractised pray'r,
My trembling tongue sincere ignored
  The aids of "sweet" and "fair."
I only said, as in me lay,
  I'd strive her "worth" to reach ;
She frowned, and turned her eyes away, —
  So much for truth in speech.

Then DELIA came. I changed my plan ;
  I praised her to her face ;
I praised her features, — praised her fan,
  Her lap-dog and her lace ;
I swore that not till Time were dead
  My passion should decay ;
She, smiling, gave her hand, and said
  'Twill last then — for a DAY.

OF HIS MISTRESS.

(After Anthony Hamilton.)

To G. S.

SHE that I love is neither brown nor fair,
　　And, in a word her worth to say,
There is no maid that with her may
　　　　Compare.

Yet of her charms the count is clear, I ween :
　　There are five hundred things we see,
And then five hundred too there be,
　　　　Not seen.

Her wit, her wisdom are direct from Heaven :
　　But the sweet Graces from their store
A thousand finer touches more
　　　　Have given.

Her cheek's warm dye what painter's brush could
　　　　note ?
　　Beside her Flora would be wan
And white as whiteness of the swan
　　　　Her throat.

240

Her supple waist, her arm from Venus came,
  Hebe her nose and lip confess,
  And, looking in her eyes, you guess
    Her name.

THE NAMELESS CHARM.

(Expanded from an Epigram of Tiron.)

STELLA, 'tis not your dainty head,
    Your artless look, I own ;
'Tis not your dear coquettish tread,
    Or this, or that, alone ;

Nor is it all your gifts combined ;
    'Tis something in your face, —
The untranslated, undefined,
    Uncertainty of grace,

That taught the Boy on Ida's hill
    To whom the meed was due ;
All three have equal charms — but still
    This one I give it to !

TO PHIDYLE.

(HOR. III., 23.)

INCENSE, and flesh of swine, and this year's
    grain,
At the new moon, with suppliant hands, bestow,
O rustic Phidyle ! So naught shall know
Thy crops of blight, thy vine of Afric bane,
And hale the nurslings of thy flock remain
Through the sick apple-tide. Fit victims grow
'Twixt holm and oak upon the Algid snow,
Or Alban grass, that with their necks must stain
The Pontiff's axe : to thee can scarce avail
Thy modest gods with much slain to assail,
Whom myrtle crowns and rosemary can please.
Lay on the altar a hand pure of fault ;
More than rich gifts the Powers it shall appease,
Though pious but with meal and crackling salt.

TO HIS BOOK.

(HOR. EP. I., 20.)

FOR mart and street you seem to pine
  With restless glances, Book of mine !
Still craving on some stall to stand,
Fresh pumiced from the binder's hand.
You chafe at locks, and burn to quit
Your modest haunt and audience fit
For hearers less discriminate.
I reared you up for no such fate.
Still, if you *must* be published, go ;
But mind, you can't come back, you know !

" What have I done ? " I hear you cry,
And writhe beneath some critic's eye ;
" What did I want ? " — when, scarce polite,
They do but yawn, and roll you tight.
And yet methinks, if I may guess
(Putting aside your heartlessness
In leaving me and this your home),
You should find favour, too, at Rome.
That is, they'll like you while you're young,
When you are old, you'll pass among

The Great Unwashed, — then thumbed and sped,
Be fretted of slow moths, unread,
Or to Ilerda you'll be sent,
Or Utica, for banishment !
And I, whose counsel you disdain,
At that your lot shall laugh amain,
Wryly, as he who, like a fool,
Thrust o'er the cliff his restive mule.
Nay ! there is worse behind.   In age
They e'en may take your babbling page
In some remotest " slum " to teach
Mere boys their rudiments of speech !

But go.   When on warm days you see
A chance of listeners, speak of me.
Tell them I soared from low estate,
A freedman's son, to higher fate
(That is, make up to me in worth
What you must take in point of birth) ;
Then tell them that I won renown
In peace and war, and pleased the town ;
Paint me as early gray, and one
Little of stature, fond of sun,
Quick-tempered, too, — but nothing more.
Add (if they ask) I'm forty-four,
Or was, the year that over us
Both Lollius ruled and Lepidus.

FOR A COPY OF HERRICK.

MANY days have come and gone,
　　Many suns have set and shone,
HERRICK, since thou sang'st of Wake,
Morris-dance and Barley-break ; —
Many men have ceased from care,
Many maidens have been fair,
Since thou sang'st of JULIA's eyes,
JULIA's lawns and tiffanies ; —
Many things are past : but thou,
GOLDEN-MOUTH, art singing now,
Singing clearly as of old,
And thy numbers are of gold !

WITH A VOLUME OF VERSE.

A BOUT the ending of the Ramadán,
 When leanest grows the famished Mussulman,
A haggard ne'er-do-well, Mahmoud by name,
At the tenth hour to Caliph OMAR came.
" Lord of the Faithful (quoth he), at the last
The long moon waneth, and men cease to fast ;
Hard then, O hard ! the lot of him must be,
Who spares to eat . . . but not for piety ! "
" Hast thou no calling, Friend ? "— the Caliph said.
" Sir, I make verses for my daily bread."
" Verse ! " — answered OMAR.   " 'Tis a dish, indeed,
Whereof but scantily a man may feed.
Go.   Learn the Tenter's or the Potter's Art, —
Verse is a drug not sold in any mart."

I know not if that hungry Mahmoud died ;
But this I know — he must have versified,
For, with his race. from better still to worse,
The plague of writing follows like a curse ;
And men will scribble though they fail to dine,
Which is the Moral of more Books than mine.

FOR THE AVERY "KNICKER-BOCKER."

(WITH ORIGINAL DRAWINGS BY G. H. BOUGHTON.)

SHADE of Herrick, Muse of Locker,
    Help me sing of Knickerbocker !

BOUGHTON, had you bid me chant
Hymns to Peter Stuyvesant !
Had you bid me sing of Wouter,
He, the onion-head, the doubter !
But to rhyme of this one, — Mocker !
Who shall rhyme to Knickerbocker ?

Nay, but where my hand must fail
There the more shall yours avail ;
You shall take your brush and paint
All that ring of figures quaint, —
All those Rip-van-Winkle jokers, —
All those solid-looking smokers,
Pulling at their pipes of amber
In the dark-beamed Council-Chamber.

Only art like yours can touch
Shapes so dignified . . . and Dutch ;
Only art like yours can show
How the pine-logs gleam and glow,
Till the fire-light laughs and passes
'Twixt the tankards and the glasses,
Touching with responsive graces
All those grave Batavian faces, —
Making bland and beatific
All that session soporific.

Then I come and write beneath,
BOUGHTON, he deserves the wreath ;
He can give us form and hue —
This the Muse can never do !

TO A PASTORAL POET.

(H. E. B.)

AMONG my best I put your Book,
O Poet of the breeze and brook !
(That breeze and brook which blows and falls
More soft to those in city walls)
Among my best : and keep it still
Till down the fair grass-girdled hill,
Where slopes my garden-slip, there goes
The wandering wind that wakes the rose,
And scares the cohort that explore
The broad-faced sun-flower o'er and o'er,
Or starts the restless bees that fret
The bindweed and the mignonette.

Then I shall take your Book, and dream
I lie beside some haunted stream ;
And watch the crisping waves that pass,
And watch the flicker in the grass ;
And wait — and wait — and wait to see
The Nymph . . . that never comes to me !

"SAT EST SCRIPSISSE."

(TO E. G., WITH A COLLECTION OF ESSAYS.)

WHEN You and I have wandered beyond
    the reach of call,
And all our Works immortal lie scattered on the
    Stall,
It may be some new Reader, in that remoter age,
Will find the present volume and listless turn the
    page.

For him I speak these verses. And, Sir (I say
    to him),
This Book you see before you, — this master-
    piece of Whim
Of Wisdom, Learning, Fancy (if you will, please,
    attend), —
Was written by its Author, who gave it to his
    Friend.

For they had worked together, been Comrades
    of the Pen;
They had their points at issue, they differed now
    and then;

251

But both loved Song and Letters, and each had
    close at heart
The hopes, the aspirations, the " dear delays " of
    Art.

And much they talked of Measures and more
    they talked of Style,
Of Form and " lucid Order," of " labour of the
    File ; "
And he who wrote the writing, as sheet by sheet
    was penned
(This all was long ago, Sir !), would read it to
    his friend.

They knew not, nor cared greatly, if they were
    spark or star ;
They knew to move is somewhat, although the
    goal be far ;
And larger light or lesser, this thing at least is
    clear,
They served the Muses truly, — their service was
    sincere.

This tattered page you see, Sir, this page alone
    remains
(Yes, — fourpence is the lowest !) of all those
    pleasant pains ;

And as for him that read it, and as for him that
    wrote,
No Golden Book enrolls them among its " Names
    of Note."

And yet they had their office. Though they to-
    day are passed,
They marched in that procession where is no first
    or last ;
Though cold is now their hoping, though they no
    more aspire,
They too had once their ardour — they handed
    on the fire.

PROLOGUES AND EPILOGUES.

PROLOGUE TO ABBEY'S EDITION OF "SHE STOOPS TO CONQUER."

IN the year Seventeen Hundred and Seventy
    and Three,
When the GEORGES were ruling o'er Britain the
    free,
There was played a new play, on a new-fashioned
    plan,
By the GOLDSMITH who brought out the *Good-
    Natur'd Man.*
New-fashioned, in truth — for this play, it appears,
Dealt largely in laughter, and nothing in tears,
While the type of those days, as the learnèd will
    tell ye,
Was the CUMBERLAND whine or the whimper of
    KELLY.
So the Critics pooh-poohed, and the Actresses
    pouted,
And the Public were cold, and the Manager
    doubted;
But the Author had friends, and they all went to
    see it.
Shall we join them in fancy? You answer, So
    be it!

Imagine yourself then, good Sir, in a wig,
Either grizzle or bob — never mind, you look big.
You've a sword at your side, in your shoes there
    are buckles,
And the folds of fine linen flap over your knuckles.
You have come with light heart, and with eyes
    that are brighter,
From a pint of red Port, and a steak at the Mitre ;
You have strolled from the Bar and the purlieus
    of Fleet,
And you turn from the Strand into Catherine
    Street ;
Thence climb to the law-loving summits of Bow,
Till you stand at the Portal all play-goers know.
See, here are the 'prentice lads laughing and
    pushing,
And here are the seamstresses shrinking and
    blushing,
And here are the urchins who, just as to-day, Sir,
Buzz at you like flies with their " Bill o' the Play,
    Sir ? "
Yet you take one, no less, and you squeeze by
    the Chairs,
With their freights of fine ladies, and mount up
    the stairs ;
So issue at last on the House in its pride,
And pack yourself snug in a box at the side.

Here awhile let us pause to take breath as we sit,
Surveying the humours and pranks of the Pit, —
With its Babel of chatterers buzzing and humming,
With its impudent orange-girls going and coming,
With its endless surprises of face and of feature,
All grinning as one in a gust of good-nature.
Then we turn to the Boxes where TRIP in his lace
Is aping his master, and keeping his place.
Do but note how the Puppy flings back with a
    yawn,
Like a Duke at the least, or a Bishop in lawn !
Then sniffs at his bouquet, whips round with a
    smirk,
And ogles the ladies at large — like a Turk.
But the music comes in, and the blanks are all
    filling,
And TRIP must trip up to the seats at a shilling ;
And spite of the mourning that most of us wear
The House takes a gay and a holiday air ;
For the fair sex are clever at turning the tables,
And seem to catch coquetry even in sables.
Moreover, your mourning has ribbons and stars,
And is sprinkled about with the red coats of Mars.

Look, look, there is WILKES ! You may tell by
    the squint ;
But he grows every day more and more like the
    print

(Ah ! HOGARTH *could* draw !) ; and behind at
   the back
HUGH KELLY, who looks all the blacker in black.
That is CUMBERLAND next, and the prim-looking
   person
In the corner, I take it, is *Ossian* MACPHERSON.
And rolling and blinking, here, too, with the rest,
Comes sturdy old JOHNSON, dressed out in his
   best ;
How he shakes his old noddle ! I'll wager a
   crown,
Whatever the law is *he's* laying it down !
Beside him is REYNOLDS, who's deaf ; and the
   hale
Fresh, farmer-like fellow, I fancy, is THRALE.
There is BURKE with GEORGE STEEVENS. And
   somewhere, no doubt,
Is the AUTHOR — too nervous just now to come
   out ;
He's a queer little fellow, grave-featured, pock-
   pitten,
Tho' they say, in his cups, he's as gay as a kitten.

But where is our play-bill ? *Mistakes of a Night !*
If the title's prophetic, I pity his plight !
She Stoops. Let us hope she won't fall at full
   length,
For the piece — so 'tis whispered — is wanting in
   strength.   260

And the humour is "low!"—you are doubtless
    aware
There's a character, even, that "dances a bear!"
Then the cast is so poor,—neither marrow nor
    pith!
Why can't they get WOODWARD or Gentleman
    SMITH!
"LEE LEWES!" Who's LEWES? The fellow
    has played
Nothing better, they tell me, than harlequinade!
"DUBELLAMY"—"QUICK,"—these are no-
    bodies. Stay, I
Believe I saw QUICK once in *Beau Mordecai.*
Yes, QUICK is not bad. Mrs. GREEN, too, is
    funny;
But SHUTER, ah! SHUTER's the man for my
    money!
He's the quaintest, the oddest of mortals, is
    SHUTER,
And he has but one fault—he's too fond of the
    pewter.
Then there's little BULKELY . . .

                But here in the middle,
From the orchestra comes the first squeak of a
    fiddle. 261

Then the bass gives a growl, and the horn makes
 a dash,
And the music begins with a flourish and crash,
And away to the zenith goes swelling and
 swaying,
While we tap on the box to keep time to the
 playing.
And we hear the old tunes as they follow and
 mingle,
Till at last from the stage comes a ting-a-ting
 tingle ;
And the fans cease to whirr, and the House for a
 minute
Grows still as if naught but wax figures were
 in it.
Then an actor steps out, and the eyes of all
 glisten.
Who is it? *The Prologue.* He's sobbing. Hush!
 listen.

*[Thereupon enters Mr. Woodward in black,
with a handkerchief to his eyes, to speak
Garrick's Prologue, after which comes the
play. In the volume for which the foregoing additional Prologue was written
the following Envoi was added.]*

L'ENVOI.

G OOD-BYE to you, KELLY, your fetters are
broken !

Good-bye to you, CUMBERLAND, GOLDSMITH has
spoken !

Good-bye to sham Sentiment, moping and mum-
ming,

For GOLDSMITH has spoken and SHERIDAN'S
coming ;

And the frank Muse of Comedy laughs in free
air

As she laughed with the Great Ones, with
SHAKESPEARE, MOLIÈRE !

PROLOGUE TO ABBEY'S "QUIET LIFE."

E VEN as one in city pent,
    Dazed with the stir and din of town,
Drums on the pane in discontent,
  And sees the dreary rain come down,
Yet, through the dimmed and dripping glass,
Beholds, in fancy, visions pass,
Of Spring that breaks with all her leaves,
Of birds that build in thatch and eaves,
Of woodlands where the throstle calls,
Of girls that gather cowslip balls,
Of kine that low, and lambs that cry,
Of wains that jolt and rumble by,
Of brooks that sing by brambly ways,
Of sunburned folk that stand at gaze,
Of all the dreams with which men cheat ·
The stony sermons of the street,
So, in its hour, the artist brain
    Weary of human ills and woes,
Weary of passion, and of pain,
    And vaguely craving for repose,
Deserts awhile the stage of strife
To draw the even, ordered life,

The easeful days, the dreamless nights,
The homely round of plain delights,
The calm, the unambitioned mind,
Which all men seek, and few men find.

EPILOGUE.

Let the dream pass, the fancy fade !
We clutch a shape, and hold a shade.
Is Peace *so* peaceful ?   Nay, — who knows !
There are volcanoes under snows.

IN after days when grasses high
O'er-top the stone where I shall lie,
Though ill or well the world adjust
My slender claim to honoured dust,
I shall not question or reply.

I shall not see the morning sky ;
I shall not hear the night-wind sigh ;
I shall be mute, as all men must
In after days !

But yet, now living, fain were I
That some one then should testify,
Saying — " He held his pen in trust
To Art, not serving shame or lust."
Will none ? — Then let my memory die
In after days !

NOTES.

NOTES.

" To brandish the poles of that old Sedan Chair!" — PAGE 7.

A FRIENDLY critic, whose versatile pen is not easy to mistake, recalls, *à-propos* of the above, the following passage from Molière, which shows that Chairmen are much the same all the world over : —

1 Porteur (prenant un des bâtons de sa chaise). *Çà, payez-nous vitement !*
Mascarille. *Quoi !*
1 Porteur. *Je dis que je veux avoir de l'argent tout à l'heure.*
Mascarille. *Il est raisonnable, celui-là*, etc.

Les Précieuses Ridicules, Sc. vii.

" It has waited by portals where Garrick has played." — PAGE 8.

According to Mrs. Carter (Smith's *Nollekens*, 1828, i. 211), when Garrick acted, the hackney-chairs often stood "all round the Piazzas [Covent Garden], down Southampton-Street, and extended more than half-way along Maiden-Lane."

" A skill Préville could not disown." — PAGE 23.

Préville was the French Foote, *circa* 1760. His gifts as a comedian were of the highest order ; and he had an extraordinary faculty for identifying himself with the parts he played. Sterne, in a letter to Garrick from Paris, in 1762, calls him " Mercury himself."

NOTES.

MOLLY TREFUSIS — PAGE 32.

The epigram here quoted from "an old magazine" is to be found in the late Lord Neaves's admirable little volume, *The Greek Anthology* (*Blackwood's Ancient Classics for English Readers*). Those familiar with eighteenth-century literature will recognize in the succeeding verses but another echo of those lively stanzas of John Gay to "Molly Mogg of the Rose," which found so many imitators in his own day. Whether my heroine is to be identified with a certain "Miss Trefusis," whose *Poems* are sometimes to be found in the second-hand booksellers' catalogues, I know not. But if she is, I trust I have done her accomplished shade no wrong.

AN EASTERN APOLOGUE. — PAGE 43.

The initials "E. H. P." are those of the late eminent (and ill-fated) Orientalist, Professor Palmer. As my lines entirely owed their origin to his translations of Zoheir, I sent them to him. He was indulgent enough to praise them warmly. It is true he found anachronisms; but as he said these would cause no disturbance to orthodox Persians, I concluded I had succeeded in my little *pastiche*, and, with his permission, inscribed it to him. I wish now that it had been a more worthy tribute to one of the most erudite and versatile scholars this age has seen.

A REVOLUTIONARY RELIC. — PAGE 48.

" 373. ST. PIERRE (Bernardin de), *Paul et Virginie*, 12mo, old calf. Paris, 1787. This copy is pierced throughout by a bullet-hole, and bears on one of the covers the words : ' *à Lucile St. A. . . . chez M Batemans, à Edmonds-Bury, en Angleterre,*' very faintly written in pencil." (Extract from Catalogue)

NOTES.

" Did she wander like that other ? " — PAGE 50.

Lucile Desmoulins. See Carlyle's *French Revolution*, Book vi. Chap. ii.

" And its tender rain shall lave it." — PAGE 52.

It is by no means uncommon for an editor to interrupt some of these revolutionary letters by a " Here there are traces of tears."

" By ' Bysshe,' his epithet." — PAGE 81.

i.e. *The Art of English Poetry*, by Edward Bysshe, 1702.

THE BOOK-PLATE'S PETITION. — PAGE 87.

These lines were reprinted from *Notes and Queries* in Mr. Andrew Lang's delightful volume *The Library*, 1881, where the curious will find full information as to the enormities of the book-mutilators.

" Have I not writ thy Laws ? " — PAGE 93.

The lines in italic type which follow, are freely paraphrased from the ancient *Code d'Amour* of the XIIth Century, as given by André le Chapelain himself.

A DIALOGUE, ETC. — PAGE 107.

This dialogue, first printed in *Scribner's Magazine* for May, 1888, was afterwards read by Professor Henry Morley at the opening of the Pope Loan Museum at Twickenham (July 31st), to the Catalogue of which exhibition it was prefixed.

" The ' crooked Body with a crooked Mind.' " — PAGE 108.

" Mens curva in corpore curvo."
Said of Pope by Lord Orrery.

"*Neither as* LOCKE *was, nor as* BLAKE." — PAGE 115.

The Shire Hall at Taunton, where these verses were read at the unveiling, by Mr. James Russell Lowell, of Miss Margaret Thomas's bust of Fielding, September 4th, 1883, also contains busts of Admiral Blake and John Locke.

"*The Journal of his middle-age.*" — PAGE 118.

It is, perhaps, needless to say that the reference here is to the *Journal of a Voyage to Lisbon*, published posthumously in February, 1755, — a record which for its intrinsic pathos and dignity may be compared with the letter and dedication which Fielding's predecessor and model, Cervantes, prefixed to his last romance of *Persiles and Sigismunda*.

CHARLES GEORGE GORDON. — PAGE 120.

These verses appeared in the *Saturday Review* for February 14th, 1885.

ALFRED, LORD TENNYSON. — PAGE 122.

These verses appeared in the *Athenæum* for October 8th, 1892.

"*With that he made a Leg.*" — PAGE 137.

"JOVE made his Leg and kiss'd the Dame,
Obsequious HERMES did the Same."

PRIOR.

"*So took his Virtù off to Cock's.*" — PAGE 137.

Cock, the auctioneer of Covent Garden, was the Christie and Manson of the last century. The leading idea of this fable, it should be added, is taken from one by Gellert.

" *Of Van's ' Goose-Pie.'* " — PAGE 139.

" At length they in the Rubbish spy
A Thing resembling a Goose Py."
    SWIFT's verses on *Vanbrugh's House*, 1706.

" *The Oaf preferred the* ' Tongs and Bones.' " — PAGE 145.

" I have a reasonable good ear in music ; let us have the tongs and the bones."
    Midsummer-Night's Dream, Act iv., Sc. i.

" *And sighed o'er Chaos wine for Stingo* " — PAGE 145.

Squire Homespun probably meant Cahors.

THE WATER-CURE. — PAGE 178.

These verses were suggested by the recollection of an anecdote in Madame de Genlis, which seemed to lend itself to eighteenth-century treatment. It was therefore somewhat depressing, not long after they were written, to find that the subject had already been annexed in the *Tatler* by an actual eighteenth-century writer, who, moreover, claimed to have founded his story on a contemporary incident. Burton, nevertheless, had told it before him, as early as 1621, in the *Anatomy of Melancholy*.

" *In Babylonian numbers hidden.*" — PAGE 180.

" — nec Babylonios
Tentaris numeros."
    HOR. i., 11.

" *And spite of the mourning that most of us wear.*" — PAGE 253.

In March, 1773, when *She Stoops to Conquer* was first

played, there was a court-mourning for the King of Sardinia
(Forster's *Goldsmith*, Book iv. Chap. 15).

" But he grows every day more and more like the print. —
Page 253.

" Mr. *Wilkes*, with his usual good humour, has been heard
to observe, that he is every day growing more and more like
his portrait by *Hogarth* (i.e. the print of May 16th, 1763]."
Biographical Anecdotes of William Hogarth, 1782,
pp. 305–6.